TEMPTED BY THE HOT CHEF

GAY ROMANCE

HOT AND SAUCY
BOOK THREE

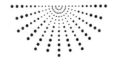

DILLON HART

PROLOGUE

MARTIN

Well, I've never kissed a Viking in a restaurant-grade kitchen before.

But from the intensity in those dark blue eyes? Yeah, it's definitely happening.

But not without some seriously dramatic moves on his part.

This isn't your run-of-the-mill kitchen-banging chef.

This is full-on six-four blond, muscled dream guy in full-on "I'll make you swoon" mode.

Bring it.

Expensive copper pots and pans clang to the floor as he sweeps one massive arm across the stainless-steel prep area.

Seriously.

If you only could see those biceps with the tattoos snaking down them...muscles coiled tense as though he's going to spring at any moment.

One second, I'm prepping for the big night of our pop-up restaurant—sold out thanks to the great buzz that the Chef-Off Competition generates—and the next, I look up to see all six-foot-four inches of a big, totally striking, totally fever-inducing guy ready to have his wicked way with me.

When I say wicked? Oh yeah.

Erik Svensson, the descendent of Vikings—and bad boy chef.

World-class sushi expert imported from the East Coast to Sin City just to make headlines as part of the Chow Channel's big Chef-Off.

Just to make things a little more complicated? He's my brother's best friend and my top rival in the event.

I'd shown up, ready to rock.

Actually, I'm lying.

I was *terrified:* my mentor—a world-famous chef in his own right—let me work my way up in his kitchen the old-fashioned way.

Sweat, tears, and a few broken dishes.

Now, I'm going head-to-head with the kinds of culinary talent they write about in big, glossy magazines I can't even pronounce, never mind read.

And then I show up at the Las Vegas casino, all kitted out for the big event.

Who's there? The guy I'd imagined this moment with a thousand times.

My brother's big, gorgeous best friend.

The guy I've been crushing on since high school.

And yeah, he's pretty fancy too.

He's worked his way around the world, heating up kitchens from the cheese-filled glory of Paris to years of studying sushi arts in Japan.

His adventures? The stuff of legends. Then he comes back to the States and goes home to Boston. Starts up some fancy place but gets tangled up with bad investors.

That's the gist anyways.

Imagine my horror-but-delight-but-fear-but-hope when I look up and see Big Sexy two lines back in the giant fake kitchen erected for the event.

Speaking of which…

Erik stands inches away from me—oh, lord, inches—his eyes darkening.

The strands of his pale blond shoulder-length hair hang free to his shoulders. Those Atlantic-blue eyes are wild with desire.

And I have three seconds to hope the doors are locked before he picks me up and sits me down on the stainless-steel table.

"Yes?"

I love a man that loves consent.

"Fuck, yes."

That's the thing I've learned from Erik.

There's a difference between "yeah, sure" and "hell, yes."

And there's a difference between "hell, yes," and "fuck, yes."

I'm making more choices in my life that are *fuck, yes.*

This fire's just getting started.

But don't let me get ahead of myself.

CHAPTER ONE

ERIK

SIX WEEKS AGO

"Mafia? Are you sure?"

I bite into my anchovy crisp, savoring the cracker's crunch and hint of smoky olive oil.

"Positive," I say, jamming a frustrated hand through my hair, shoving the pale-blond strands out of my face. I need a damn haircut. "Anthony's got a rap sheet a mile long. It's not good news, my friend."

A pinch more salt. That's what this dish needs. And next time, I'll sear the fish just a second longer, pushing the appetizer from great to divine.

The Shark Fin has a reputation for only the best, right?

It's a spur-of-the-moment lunch with my college roommate and best friend, Chris, on the terrace outside The Shark Fin, the upscale bar and sushi joint I own in downtown Boston.

It's the perfect time to try to a new dish before I roll it out to demanding customers on tonight's menu.

Today's full of surprises, and the sunshine is blaringly strong, considering March is usually frigid enough to keep snow from melting.

Chris's arrival from New York is a good surprise. It's been too long since I've seen him or had a chance to do more than fire off hurried texts. Frankly, the slight potbelly he's developed after trading his line cook job for an office job shocks me. He's normally such a fitness freak.

Something's going on down in New York, but I'll have to find out more about that later. Right now, I'm balls-deep in my own problems.

"I've got Dad bod now," Chris offers in defense to my raised eyebrow. I don't have the heart to remind him he isn't a dad.

And the message this morning from Benny, the one that's still saved on my phone. Yeah, that was a surprise too.

Maybe it shouldn't be. Anthony, my restaurant's top investor, always seems dodgy to me. Shoes impeccably shined, even in the middle of winter. Never clear about exactly what industry he's in.

Once, I caught Anthony threatening someone—a chubby, sweaty guy in a tracksuit—who occasionally shares his regular booth in the corner.

I mean, come on. A tracksuit?

All signs point to Mafia; but it's still hard to swallow.

"Like the movies?" Chris can't fully grasp it, either. He steals the last of the cod croquettes, running it through the lemon cream sauce. "Italian?"

"Full on Sopranos shit, yeah." I sip my water, watching the people passing by through dark sunglasses.

Any one of them could be Mafia. Maybe there's a whole army of them, Anthony's guys, watching the restaurant day and night. Maybe someone's watching us right now, wondering if a six-foot-four, blond Swedish guy with a fish restaurant is a threat or not.

That's fine. I'm descended from fucking Vikings. I eat fear for breakfast. At least, that's what I keep telling myself.

"You're in Boston. Isn't the mob here usually Irish?" Chris points out, reasonably.

"His name is Anthony Napali," I give my friend a hard look. "What do you think?"

"Benny says he's using the restaurant to launder money?" Chris shakes his head, pulling his phone out of his pocket. "Fuck, that's awful. What if it's really dirty money? What if it's weapons? Or cocaine? Or, even worse—"

"I invited you here to give me comfort, not add to my list of reasons to freak out." I keep my voice light, but my stomach is a bundle of nerves.

He's just voicing what I've been thinking all morning.

"I thought you invited me here to taste-test your weird little experiments." Chris gestures at the spread of now-empty dishes. They're a regular occurrence, these meals where one of us cooks for the other, testing new recipes and flavor combinations.

Lately, it seems like this is the only way to get Chris to leave his beloved Brooklyn and come home to Boston.

"Well, that too." I pull shoulder-length hair into a knot; it's already messy and will just get messier once The Shark Fin opens for the night.

"So, what do you think?"

Chris finishes sending a text, then surveys the dirty plates. "Hmmm. Well, there was a lot of parsley on the bruschetta. Kind of overpowered the basil—"

"Not the food," I cut in. "The Mafia, asshole. What do I know about the mob?"

Chris shrugs. "Anthony's been your top investor for three years now. You turned a profit in six months thanks to him. You really want to dump someone that resourceful?"

I hate it when Chris is so pragmatic.

"But he's not a good man." I keep my voice down.

Maybe I have Viking's blood, ten generations back, but while my great-great-grandparents fought their way from Sweden to America on the edge of a sword, I'm not violent.

I'm a foodie, for fuck's sake.

It's a passion that's taken me around the world. I studied in Japan for years, working under a master sushi chef. I interned in Greece, bussed tables in France, and ran a Costa Rican beachfront fish food shack, handing out fish tacos to tourists soaking up the sun.

All I want to do now is run my restaurant and keep my nose clean. I don't want to get involved in anything dangerous or seedy.

I'll defend what's mine. I'm not afraid when life gets raw. But my days of bar fights and dangerous living are behind me. At least, I thought they were.

Chris leans across the table, glancing over his shoulder before furtively whispering, "Think he's ever buried bodies here?"

"Stop it." Still, I can't help but snort.

"Sorry," Chris suddenly says, answering his phone.

His voice takes on a fake cheerful tone. "Hey, bro. Everything okay?"

Chris's brother, Martin—I immediately straighten, even though he's across the country going to school in Las Vegas.

But it's just an instinctive reaction whenever I hear his name. There's something about him, even though he's Chris's kid brother.

Cute? Hell, yeah. Funny? For sure. But something less definable always pulls at me when I'm near him, and it's hard to slam it down. But then I always tell myself he's Chris's little brother and that I'm not going there.

Chris finishes his conversation, shaking his head as he tucks the phone back in his pocket. "He's going through a break-up. A bad one."

"He's calling you for emotional support?" I snark.

But I'm already getting pissed.

"If only he had a real Mafia gangster in his circle," Chris retorts. "Then he could take care of his asshole ex-boyfriend, no problem."

Anger rises so hard and fast. Thinking of Martin stuck dealing with a bad ex—whatever that means—pisses me off more than I care to think about. My eyes take in the symphony of midday traffic as images of him linger in my mind.

"What are you going to do?" Chris finally asks. "For real."

My brain is dragged back to the present, leaving the delicious Martin of my imagination for later.

I've been racking my brain for the one solution that will get me what I want—my restaurant, free and clear from any ties to anyone, but most especially the mob.

"I've got to buy Anthony out. It's the only way to remove him from the situation without involving the authorities."

"And how much has he sunk into this place?"

I give Chris the number.

He whistles. "That is a lot of sashimi."

"More than I've got available in liquid cash, with everything I have tied up in my restaurants," I agree. "Which is why I'm totally fucked."

Millions.

"Hang on." Chris takes out his phone again and mine buzzes. "I saw this the other day and was going to send it to you."

The text takes me to the website for the Chow Channel.

"Celebrity Chef-Off Competition!" the page reads. "The best and the brightest face-off in a series of themed challenges. Audition now!"

"Take a look at that prize money."

It's too good to be true—ten million dollars would go to the winner, more than enough to get me out of this Mafia mess without having to sell off a restaurant I love.

Auditions are next week, in select cities around the country—and Boston's on the list.

Perfect. I start making plans for how to get the funds to make The Shark Fin mine for good.

CHAPTER TWO

ERIK

"Order up!" The silver bell on the pick-up line chimes, but I don't have time to watch the plates of seafood appetizers heading out of the kitchen. I'm already whirling around, back to the stovetop, making sure these cranberry oyster bites don't burn.

It's mid-shift on a Thursday evening, and The Shark Fin is packed.

The upscale half of the sushi bar is filled with the after-work crowd desperate for a little joy in otherwise jam-packed schedules, or awkward couples on first dates. Those are always the most painful to watch. Meanwhile, the guys from the financial district stand elbow-deep in the other side of the restaurant, a television over the bar turned to a sports game.

Every once in a while, the entire restaurant erupts in cheers.

I serve up the next platter of appetizers. The finest fish caught in the Atlantic just today, served up tonight to a crowd with mixed levels of appreciation.

In a few short days, I'm heading to a place where they worship flavor, texture, concept.

And if all goes well after that, I'll have the money I need to buy The Shark Fin outright—and that television over the bar is the first thing going.

"Pick up!" I bark, just in time to see Anthony Napali stroll into the kitchen like it was his own office.

It's been six weeks since I learned that Anthony, my biggest investor, is actually in the Mafia. The more digging I do, the clearer it becomes Anthony's into some scary stuff—which means that The Shark Fin, as a funnel for all of the Mafia's dirty money, is by default involved, too.

No fucking way I'm getting caught up in that and letting this guy's choices destroy my life.

"Anthony!" I plaster a grin on his face. "I didn't know you were coming in tonight."

"Neither did I, but the thought of your seafood gnocchi had me walking here with my eyes closed." Napali's a slick-looking man with a tough-guy accent and black hair greased to his scalp. I've never seen him adorned in anything but head-to-toe black. When I met the guy, Anthony already looked the part of a gangster—but I'd been so excited to open The Shark Fin, I'd taken his money without so much as a second thought.

My other restaurants had investors, after all. Just typically people I knew better, or large holding companies. When the perfect space opened up that would let me get back to Boston, back to my first love of making sushi, I'd acted fast. The support of a local businessman had seemed like a good thing. What's the old saying? Now, I'm repenting at leisure.

"Coming right up." I dish up his favorite entrée.

"I also wanted to talk to you," Anthony says, grabbing a stool at the edge of the counter. "Have you seen the numbers lately?"

I have. Despite the packed dining room, numbers are down. Nothing disastrous, not yet—restaurants are difficult businesses to sustain, after all, and have ups and downs—but The Shark Fin operating close to the line makes the reality that I needed Napali's money that much starker.

"Perfect timing, then." Anthony reaches into his pocket, pulling out a crumpled white envelope bulging with cash. "How about another allotment? I've got some cash I need to invest someplace, or else Uncle Sam will be on my ass. A hundred grand, right there."

"Anthony," I say carefully. "I just don't know if another investment is what we need right now."

It's important to be smart. Even more so when Anthony frowns, his eyes glinting with suspicion.

I don't want to call Anthony out on his Mafia connections—now's the time to keep my cards close to my chest while I arrange to remove Anthony from my business dealings.

"What are you talking about?" Anthony furrows his eyebrows. "You need a cash injection, fast. And look what I brought, right here—oh, God."

The man pauses to take a bite of the gnocchi. "You swear you're not Italian? Not even a little bit?"

"Swedish." I shrug. "Both sides."

"No, you must have an Italian somewhere in your family, way back," Anthony insists. "No one else can make gnocchi like that."

A server walks in and punches a new order into the computer; seconds later, the order appears on my screen.

"Listen," Anthony says. "I know you need to get back to work but listen to me. You're talented and you're well on your way to a global empire. Take the money."

Frustration is rising. I don't like having to dance around things. "I'm going to Vegas next week. To a chef competition."

Anthony raises his eyebrows. "Is that so?"

"It's a big deal." I shrug at the mobster. "A deal with the Chow Channel could mean big things for The Shark Fin."

Anthony makes a noncommittal hand gesture.

"This looks like a solid investment in your future. I'll be rooting for you. In the meantime, take the cash. Put it toward bills. You'll pay me back when the time comes, I have no doubts about that."

Is it me or did that sound vaguely ominous?

It doesn't matter. My plan's right on schedule. I'll blow it out of the water at the Chef-Off Competition. Now, I just have to fly to Vegas, kill it, and I'll have the cash in hand to buy Napali out.

And then, I have ever bigger plans. For today, I settle for getting Napali out the door without taking dirty money and without getting stabbed in the process.

CHAPTER THREE

ERIK

Martin.

Martin Slade, Chris's kid brother.

Holy shit.

Only now he's no kid—he's all grown-up. It's hard to keep my eyes off him.

We're in one of the event areas of an iconic, high-end Las Vegas casino hosting the Chef-Off Competition, and some producer's going over the schedule for the week.

Starting tomorrow, twenty chefs will complete a daily challenge, the judges eliminating the least favorite dishes. By the last day, Saturday, just two of us will be left to compete in front of a live audience and take the prize.

Easy enough.

At least, it should be. All superfluous information. Yet no matter how much I want that ten million, I can't keep my eyes off Martin's copper-red curls, the handful of freckles sprinkled across his nose, the dimple in his left cheek. The last time I saw him, that'd been a few years ago and he'd have been cute, but young.

Now though? Absolute stunner.

Heads-turn-when-he-enters-a-room stunning. That has all the blood flow in my body racing for my junk, and has me fucking distracted on the day I can't afford—literally—not to completely pay attention. My eyes trace down his body; he's got on chef's whites, same as every other chef in the room, but no one else has a body like his. His shoulders are narrow but muscled, then his waist curves into a tight cinch before slightly angling back out again in a pair of slender, sexy hips.

He's got the body of a Greek God, one of the young ones, his long legs making my cock twitch.

Jesus, how the fuck is this dreamboat related to Chris? And how the fuck did Chris not tell me his baby brother is in the same event as me?

Something in my chest flutters as Martin makes eye contact. Fuck, now he's caught me staring. He lifts his eyebrows and purses his sensuous peach lips in surprise. When the producer wraps up orientation, he heads straight for me.

"Well, well, Erik Svensson." He says my name like I'm trouble—or like I'm going to be in trouble. It's every schoolboy's bossy school principal fantasy wrapped up in a fucking chef's coat, and it's taking all my self-restraint not to fall to my knees.

"Martin. Good to see you." I go for chill, even though he's setting me on fire.

He steps toward me, arms wide, wrapping me in a chaste hug. Breathing in his heady woodsy scent, I try not to think about him pressed up against my body. But those dangerous muscles are full impact against me, leaving me praying he doesn't notice my hard-on.

"Didn't know you'd be here. Chris didn't mention it."

I'm seriously going to fucking kill him. Although, what will I say? *How dare you not tell me your hot little brother was going to be here?* Yeah, that'll go over well.

"Chris..." Martin rolls wide, sparking eyes with a playful chuckle. "Chris can't remember anything unless it's happening an hour from now. I told him weeks ago that I'd made it into the competition."

"You've been working in a restaurant these last few years?" In every conversation I've ever had with Chris that mentioned Martin, the only detail he could recall was that he'd been through a messy breakup.

Is it wrong to silently rejoice, knowing he's single?

"At the Wish Café." Martin runs a hand casually through his red curls, cutting his glance up at me. He knows what I'll say.

"The Wish Café. Frank's place?" Frank McIntosh is one of those rare chefs who manages to outlive every generation of food trends and makes big money doing it. "He's a legend. No one better to learn from."

"He sure is." Martin smiles coyly, and my heart slams in my chest. When he smiles, his dimple appears, so adorably sexy I can't stop looking at it. "See you around, Svensson."

"See you, Slade." It wasn't until I'd cooled off in the spring air that I stopped to see the implication.

Frank's a legend, absolutely—and legendary chefs only hire incredibly talented prodigies to work under their wings.

Martin must be one hell of a chef, then.

And if this competition's the solution to getting The Shark Fin back from the mob, I'll have to defeat him—

Defeat him or fuck him. I'm not sure which I want to do more.

"Stop," I growl to myself, heading back to my hotel room. "That's Chris's little brother. He's off-limits."

But all night, I struggle to get that adorable dimple out of my mind.

CHAPTER FOUR

MARTIN

When I'd gone into work on a random Tuesday six weeks ago, two things surprised me.

First, Frank was there.

Frank McIntosh, legendary chef with four Michelin stars under his belt and multiple restaurants all around the world, had settled in Las Vegas, returning to the hole-in-the-wall café that had been his very first venture.

Most people assumed it was because Frank was retiring, or because he wanted to be near family after a lifetime of globe-trotting and trail-blazing.

But I know the truth. Frank has multiple sclerosis, and ever since he turned sixty a few years ago, his symptoms have been progressing.

Most days, he can't hold a knife steady.

But that morning when I swing into the kitchen to gear up for the weekday Las Vegas brunch crowd—God bless Sin City and the steady seven-nights-a-week drinking—there stands Frank, rinsing berries in the sink.

"What's going on?" I ask quickly after making sure everything's okay. Usually, Frank swings by Wish Café once or twice a week to make sure everything's running in tip-top shape, but it's unusual to see him hands-on in the kitchen.

"Everything's dandy, or it will be once you take a look at this."

Frank doesn't quite look at me when he answers, pushing printouts at me with wet fingers. I pick them up and skim fast: the Chow Channel is hosting a big celebrity chef competition. Frank wants me to enter.

"I'm not good enough for this," I snap, tying on my apron and pinning errant curls away from my face with a bandana. "I've only been working here for a few years —I don't even have any formal training."

Making recipes someone shows me how to do and where they then relentlessly train me until I get them right? Yeah, sure, no problem. But I'm not some culinary genius. Hell, I'm not Erik Svensson with his constant experimentation and passion for new creations.

My cheeks color just thinking of his name.

"What do you call this?" Frank gestures from him to me. "The best training anywhere. I've taught you everything I know. You're better than most of the idiots they graduate from culinary school these days."

That's Frank. Subtle as hell.

I turn bright red, cracking eggs into a bowl for the signature stuffed French toast. Never can keep my feelings from showing when I blush. Frank hates that cooking's become such an elitist occupation. He hates training in classrooms instead of on cooking lines in local greasy spoons. Honestly, that's why I love working with him: because he's not pretentious and has a down-to-earth approach to cooking that reminds me of long-ago days, baking boxed brownies with my mom in our tiny apartment kitchen.

It'd been magical, and my chest pulls tight at the thought of those simpler times.

Of the days when my family was together. I've been on my own way too long.

"You'll spank every one of them," Frank grumbles. "You're ready for this. But if you need real motivation, take a look at the prize."

My eyes widen when I see the competition prize and instantly know what I'd do with the money if I won.

Frank made decent money in his heyday as a world-renowned chef, but most of it, he invested back into his businesses. Now he relies on the profits from the Wish Café. He won't be able to retire, not without a source of income.

And I want to give that to him.

Ever since my parents died, I've always been searching for someone to inspire me. The aunt who raised me and Chris disengaged completely once we graduated from high school, and most of my bosses were more interested in getting me to work as many hours as possible for as little pay as possible than in teaching me anything or giving a shit about my future.

But Frank? He's different.

Frank's taken me under his wing and treated me like a son. Nearly every good thing in my life these days, such as the home I found in Las Vegas, the career I've grown to love… I owe them all to Frank.

I decided that day to win the Chef-Off competition and buy the Wish Café so Frank could finally retire.

And now here I am, entering the big, fancy casino space for the first challenge.

Once I saw the names on the roster—I'm talking household names, cookbook authors, people who show up to cook on TV shows—I knew I stood not a chance in hell. Then, by some miracle, I'd landed first place in the Las Vegas competition and gone on to the finals.

Now, as I take my place alongside all the sleek silver counters in the massive kitchen the Chow Channel's erected for the week—there's nothing like a little Vegas showmanship—I'm suffering a serious case of imposter syndrome.

All the other contestants are from Michelin-starred restaurants. Years of training, all sorts of accolades under their belts.

And I'm just some random dork lucky enough to get chosen by Frank McIntosh.

As I look around the space, I catch Erik's eye, and his grin from the counter three rows behind leaves me warm and feverish. Fuck, that man!

Huge. Six four, with muscles that ripple even under his chef's coat. Pale blond hair and blue eyes and those fucking cheekbones. Basically, if your dream guy's a Viking who cooks? Erik Svennson checks all the boxes. Just thinking about it leaves my mouth dry.

My brother had mentioned that Erik was auditioning, but I'd been so shocked to be chosen for the competition that I'd completely forgotten.

Until I saw him yesterday.

Look, I've always had a little crush on him—how could I not? He's tall, thick with muscles like a Viking, his long hair always loosely pulled back. Those unusual dark blue eyes, the color of the stormy Atlantic, always have a little bit of a wicked twinkle when he glances at me—and once or twice, I've caught him staring at my butt.

I like imagining what he would do with it if we were alone. Does he imagine the same thing?

Then it's not like I don't spend time glancing at his broad shoulders, the thickness of his tattooed biceps, wondering what he looks like with his shirt off. Wondering if I'll ever have a chance to find out?

Erik winks at me as the announcers settle everyone down, and I face the front with an energetic smile. Frank's not here to vouch for me today.

I've got to stand on my own two feet—and anytime I need a fresh burst of confidence again, I'll just look back at Erik.

I want to impress the judges, of course, but if I could impress him, too—well, that'd be double the win.

We've always gotten along so well.

But even as the thought strikes, I'm backpedaling. For one, my brother would kill me. Erik's been his best friend for years. But Chris clearly and sharply told me on more than one occasion that Erik's got a wild side, and loves his playboy lifestyle...and that he used to travel the world and had adventures too crazy for my brother to even repeat.

Besides, I'm not his type. The reminder is that my chef's whites are tight against my still adolescent shaped body. Compared to some of these other ripped men, I'm scrawny, nerdy. Don't think for a minute that I hate every inch of my damned body, and I've certainly known my share of men that liked it just fine. I'm just pretty sure I'm not the kind of guy that makes sexy Swedish chefs get all hot and bothered.

I should probably stop picturing him naked, then, and me digging my nails into his chiseled back.

Still, I can't help it. He's so damn sexy. Besides, it's like desserts: if you can't eat them, sometimes just imagining the sweetness rolling over your tongue, the creamy texture, the deliciousness filling you...It's maybe not quite the same, but still pretty damn good.

"Welcome, contestants, to the Chow Channel's first ever Chef-Off Competition!"

Rodney Randall, a cheesy game-show host in a pressed blue suit, introduces the challenge to the cameras whirring around the room on levers and cranes and lifts.

I focus on his instructions, trying to ignore the fact that I'll be on film—every little mistake magnified for an audience to pick apart. Can't worry about that.

Right now, I need to focus.

The judges are introduced—five in total, each one a bigger-named chef than the last. I'm starstruck to be in the same room, breathing the same air as the greatest living sushi chef alive, Hiroko Motomori. Astonishing to think he'll be eating something I've created.

Even as the competition takes shape, it's hard to keep my eyes forward. I feel the weight of Erik's stare behind me and imagine those dark blue eyes sweeping the proceedings, those strong hands getting ready to work magic when the heat turns up. A shiver runs down my spine.

"Time to present the first challenge!" The host makes a big show of reaching into a box, as corny dramatic music pipes in.

Basically, it's fucking perfect for the late-night food shows on the Chow Channel that I watch for hours when I'm unwinding late at night. But in person? A little surreal.

The ingredient for the first challenge—a single egg.

"Many of you will be tempted to hide behind flashy ingredients and trendy techniques!" Rodney croons. "You'll hide poor flavor profiles or you'll overstretch yourselves—well, don't! We're not interested in ostentatious presentations. There are three criteria: how good does it taste, how well does it follow our theme, and how skillfully has it been executed?"

One egg.

A single dish.

Rapid-fire ideas, things I can make, ingredients to grab.

But I can't help but remember the first time I met Frank.

I didn't know he was the legendary chef Frank McIntosh; I just thought he was some slightly irreverent old guy killing time at the counter of the diner where I waited tables.

One of the line cooks quit the day before, no replacement in sight, so I stepped in to cook the eggs.

I dropped off Frank's dish: a simple mushroom omelet with pickled red onions and Gruyere cheese.

He'd taken one bite, peered up at me, almost warily. "You cooked this?"

I'd shrugged, afraid he'd ask to talk to the manager—that I'd put my job on the line by stepping in to cook. Getting fired was a real possibility if someone didn't like their meal. To say money was tight and I couldn't afford to get fired? An understatement.

"Where did you learn to cook like this?" Frank snapped.

I shrugged. "I cook like this all the time. It's just an omelet, but all food should taste good, shouldn't it?"

Frank did ask to see the manager—not to have me fired, but to inform him I was quitting to go work for him. The manager did know who Frank was and stuttered congratulations as I'd stood there, stumped.

One egg.

Simple, yet tasty.

Easy enough.

The buzzer sounds, so loud my ears sting. I dash to the pantry, fighting the other contestants for what I need.

Thirty minutes later, I throw my hands in the air, exhilaration from the post-cooking rush slamming through my body. What I'd made? Something I'd serve at Wish any day, just with a bit more flare. Some paprika, a little Irish butter. The flavor twists that bring favorites to life.

Contestants walk their egg dishes up to the judges' table. As I take my place in the line-up, stomach jumbling with nerves, a familiar voice whispers intimately in my ear: "How'd you do?"

Erik.

He's looking every inch the Viking warrior, grinning happily as he nudges in beside me. "I think I did all right. You?" I go for nonchalant.

A piece of his long whitish-blond hair tumbles free of its knot when he shrugs. It takes every ounce of my self-control not to reach up and tuck it behind his ear. "All right, I think. We'll find out soon enough, I guess."

Judges grab their silverware, taking tastes of the contestants' offerings. Maybe it's the heat from all the ranges. Maybe it's the fact that my future and Frank's are both hanging in the balance of one single egg. Maybe it's Erik, throwing Viking pheromones that I'm susceptible to at this proximity.

Whatever it is, I'm feeling bold. Brave. A little reckless.

"Want to get a bite to eat after this? We'll either celebrate our victory or drown our sorrows."

Surprise washes over the handsome lines of his face, and there's just enough hesitation that my stomach drops. This wasn't a good idea. But then he surprises me.

"Deal," Erik says. Those eyes and their wicked twinkle.

Then we're both quiet as the judges call the contestants forward to explain our dishes.

Well, at least now I have a date. Win or lose, I have something to look forward to.

CHAPTER FIVE

ERIK

"**T**o the best damn coddled eggs that have ever been coddled in the history of the world." I lift my glass to toast Martin, the star of the day.

I am already a little buzzed.

My compliment is sloppy—but Martin beams across the table anyway.

I'm not lying. I tasted the dish he served the judges. No wonder he made the top three in this first round.

"And to you," Martin adds, keeping his glass in the air. "Your eggs may have been in purgatory, but you certainly are not."

I bow my head slightly, accepting his praises. I served eggs in purgatory, making a savory, slightly spicy tomato base, then baking my egg with basil and oregano.

Both Martin and I head back tomorrow for the next challenge, along with the other eight chefs who've made it to the next round.

Hell of an end to the first challenge, and now I'm sharing a table with the most gorgeous guy in the competition. All I want to do is push aside the platters of sushi we're eating and kiss him. But then the elation of the day tamps now as I remember a fact that dampens my desire to make him mine—

Chris's brother.

Chris, my very best friend. He'll be pissed if I hit on Martin.

I should focus on the competition anyway, instead of on the way his shirt dips low enough to show the smattering of freckles across his chest. It's easy for me to imagine the way his skin probably flushes every time he cums. My mouth goes dry at the thought, my eyes snapping up to his face.

"Cut-throat. Ten contestants gone in one day," Martin says as he lifts a piece of sashimi to his mouth with chopsticks.

His lips: full, soft, perfectly peach. His tongue darts out and—

Thank God this table blocks the hard tent in my pants. "Just stay off the wrong side of the chopping block."

His dimple is showing, but his eyes are serious, burning blue against the red of his hair. "Why'd you audition? The prize money?"

The server tops off our waters, and I wait until she leaves before I say, "I have my reasons: ten million. Money is money."

He nods, carefully placing more wasabi between a ball of rice and a sliver of yellowtail. I force myself to look away from his mouth, wondering what his lips would taste like.

I don't mention anything about the Mafia—I don't want to overwhelm him with the weird problems of my life. I keep thinking that the Mafia is just a punchline in a movie, or else something that died out with the third Godfather movie. But they're very real and if I don't win this cooking competition, getting them out of my business for good is going to be a challenge.

"What about you?" I prod. "Why'd you audition?"

He glances up at the ceiling, thinking about his answer. "The money. Actually, it's less about the money and more about what I want to do with it."

He glances up at me from under his eyelashes, and I lean closer, showing him I'm listening.

"It's Frank," he says quietly. "He's not doing well. He's in the beginning stages of MS, and so he can't really work at the Wish Café. He's relied on me for a lot these last few years."

Martin pauses, biting his bottom lip, and in the desire to bite his bottom lip for him, preferably while he is spreading his legs on top of my lap, I almost miss my cue to nod at him and say, "Go on."

I'm just completely distracted by how alluring this man is. I can't remember the last time someone held my attention so completely.

"If I win the money, I'll buy the Wish Café from him so he can retire. It's Frank McIntosh—he's been in the industry for so long, given so much back to the community. I just want to make sure he's taken care of."

I am silent for a moment, letting the noise and clatter of the sushi restaurant wash around us.

Well, fuck. That's a much nobler pitch than "My funds are tied up in investments and this seems like a decent way to buy my restaurant out from under the Mafia's thumb."

I need to win this competition.

I'm counting on that money.

But for the first time since I auditioned, I realize other people will have good reasons for fighting to win, too.

It sucks to think of Frank struggling with his health. That man's an inspiration, as is everything Martin says about him giving back. Hell, I'd attended a cooking training he put on here in Vegas years ago.

But back to Martin. His eyes get wide and his voice trembles just a bit.

He's obviously taking this hard. But he's clearly got a big heart. A big fucking heart. A fighter's heart. Something about this gorgeous, statuesque man—a god in the kitchen—also being so giving hits me hard.

"I didn't know that," I offer after a moment. "About Frank."

"Most people don't." Martin stares hard at his plate.

I need to change the subject. Take us back to lighter territory. "Seriously, did you see some of the things the judges had to taste?"

"Absolutely abysmal." Martin grins. "The veggie scramble? The floppy eggs Benedict?"

"Amateurs." I drain my cup and set it down. "Don't worry, we're going to smoke them all. It'll be down to the two of us, mark my words."

A wicked grin stretches my lips. "And then," I finish playfully, "I'll take it easy on you, for Frank's sake.

You're damn right that he's a pillar of the community—
he deserves to enjoy the rest of his life after all the hard
work he's done for other chefs."

I've had a bit too much sake, so I don't notice that
Martin's not smiling back.

Not at first.

But when his blank stare turns cold and his blue eyes
stop sparkling, I realize what I said.

Fuck. Fuck my cocky brain, fuck my insensitive
bullshit.

"Martin, I say quickly. "I didn't mean that."

"You'll go easy on me?" he spits out every word like it's
venom. "What, because there's no way I could possibly
win without your help? It's a miracle I made it this far
on my own."

My insides hollow out.

"Absolutely not, Martin. I'm drunk and I'm a shit and I
didn't mean that."

I didn't—not at all.

"I don't need you or anyone to go easy on me," he fires
back, grabbing the bag holding his chef's knives and his
whites. "Life has never gone easy on me, and I think
I've done pretty well on my own."

He throws a wad of bills onto the table. "I don't need you to bring anything but your A-game. See you tomorrow, Chef."

That last word comes out sharp enough to stick right into my heart. I make to stand up, follow after him, but he's already out the door.

"Martin, wait!" My words fall on deaf ears as he leaves the restaurant without another word.

A couple at the table next to me glances over with pity in their eyes; I sink back into my chair and exhale.

I blew it. I absolutely blew it.

And what am I thinking, saying something like that?

Martin doesn't need my help winning this competition; I've tasted his dishes. They're the products of a truly skilled and instinctive chef—whereas I've been lucky to have scraped into the top three. And I know he and Chris have had to fight, unjustly hard, for everything they got after their parents died. He's poised to be a winner and doesn't need any of my bullshit.

Even if I was just trying to be playful.

Sometimes, in some things, you just don't fucking joke about.

But even though Frank McIntosh is a master and a pillar in the cooking world, I have my own problems. That prize money is the what's going to let me buy The

Shark Fin from the Mafia investor who's got his hand around my throat—

But all that still pales in comparison to what really haunts me—the look on Martin's face when I insulted him.

The betrayal.

The anger.

I never want to make him feel that way again, cooking competition or no.

It felt earlier tonight like something was growing between us, something bigger than the Chow Channel, bigger than ten million dollars.

Or maybe it's just the booze talking.

There's only one way to find out.

Something's on the chair where Martin sat—his black coat. He was so pissed that he stormed off without it. I pick it up, inhaling his woodsy scent.

I get out my phone and fire off a text. "Hey, Chris? Your brother forgot his coat and I want to bring it to him. Can you tell me where his apartment is?"

CHAPTER SIX

MARTIN

The nerve of him.

The absolute nerve.

I'm so heated from my rage, I don't even realize that I've left my coat at the sushi restaurant until I'm already fumbling with my keys outside my apartment door. By then I'm exhausted, I don't even give a fuck.

How dare he suggest he needs to take it easy on me so I can win?

Didn't he see me standing there in the top three of this round, right next to him?

I open my door and throw my stuff onto my couch before slumping onto the cushions sideways. I'm full of sushi, I'm pissed at Erik, and I'm still horny as hell—

he'd released his hair from its knot and it fell over his shoulders in gentle waves, perfectly matching the hint of a beard growing on his chin.

My own personal Viking...

Jesus, despite all the reasons I have not to, I'd been ready to jump into the sack with him.

So what if it was a terrible idea? So what if we live across the country from each other, that I'm definitely not his type, and that my brother would kill us if he found out? A one-night fling, one chance to just enjoy his raw masculinity. As I'd sipped sake, I watched the way his handsome face relaxed, the way every fucking eye in the place was glued to him and he never even noticed.

All those years flirting with him, listening extra hard whenever Chris mentioned Erik's name, the shock of seeing him at the orientation for the Chef-Off.

But he's blown it now.

Saying the absolute wrong thing.

Typical fucking arrogant asshole; the handsome ones are all the same.

The worst part, though—I think as I kick off my shoes —is how right he is. It's not like he'd meant it maliciously. It just kicked me in the gut because it echoed my thoughts.

As soon as the first round of the competition ended, I knew I was in over my head.

It's one thing to help Frank run the Wish Café, even though I don't have any formal training.

It's another to be in that room with all those superstars. They know the right way to handle their knives, the flavor profiles of random and exotic ingredients, they eat at the finest restaurants in the world. Know all the trends.

I'm not one of them.

I cook the food I know how to cook, and nothing more.

And when Erik said that thing at the restaurant, it's like he peeled back my skin and saw my deepest, darkest fears—that no matter how hard I work, no matter how hard I fight, I'll never be good enough.

I sigh and tug off my shirt as I walk to the bathroom. Just thinking about that conversation has my blood boiling. Time for a bath. The only thing that really helps me relax.

It's the reason I'd gotten the slightly more expensive apartment, still tiny by Las Vegas standards, but with a huge soak tub. Not quite a hotel model, but close enough that it makes me think the developers scored a few on the cheap when they built the place.

Soothe my muscles, calm my mind, cool my temper...

I slide into the hot water; nestling against the tub and closing my eyes, I need to relieve the pressure I'm feeling a bit.

Real-life Erik may well have pissed me off, but the imaginary one in my mind can apologize, offer to make it up to me, kneel before me and nuzzle his softly scruffy face between my legs...

My cock stirs in the water.

Erik is so tantalizingly hot, if he showed up now saying he was sorry, I'd probably still fuck him.

The thought makes me snort. Like that guy, with his Viking-sized ego and everything else, would even apologize!

My hand wanders over to my member, and begins stroking, all the tension leaving my body. Imagining Erik deep-kissing me, trailing down my neck to my naked chest—

Someone knocks on my door. Pounds on it actually.

My eyes open wide, my heart jolting.

"Hold on," I call as I grab my towel.

Shit. Whoever this is, perfect timing. It's probably just the neighbor's takeout going to the wrong place again.

Drying off as quickly as I can, I barely give myself time to tie my robe around me as I get to the door.

I peer out the peephole, and shock zips through me.

Erik.

"Martin, I want to talk to you," he rumbles through the door. "And I have your coat."

Why haven't I noticed how deep his voice is, before?

My face is burning hot—not with my earlier fury, though I'd be completely justified. I'm hot because I was touching myself in the bath while thinking about him, and right before I'd climaxed, I'd somehow conjured him here.

"I wanted to apologize," Erik goes on, the deep notes of his voice playing across my skin and sending shivers down my spine. "I don't know what I was thinking, saying such a stupid thing."

What would happen if I opened the door and started kissing him for real?

Would he kiss me back?

Would he let me lead him over to the couch, and recite his apology while I undressed him?

"You're a brilliant chef, and you deserve to be in this competition," Erik continues. "Look, if I was putting money on one person to take the whole thing, it'd be you."

Something within me deflates.

A brilliant chef.

That's all I am.

And Erik might respect me as a competitor, but he'll never be attracted to me the way I'm attracted to him. Of course not. What the hell was I thinking? I'd asked him to dinner. And of course, he'd say yes. He's my brother's best friend. It's the normal, friendly thing to do.

That—something else—that charge I feel when I'm with him? Of course, I do. He's a six-foot-four strapping Viking with the bluest eyes I've ever seen. He's friendly. Funny. Easy going. I'm not feeling that because he's directing something at me.

I'm feeling that because I'm a living, breathing, gay man. If I'm honest, every woman in the place—and half the guys too—had their eyes locked on Erik. I'd just gotten swept up. He could have anyone he wanted and he knew it.

My body is cool enough now. Most of my desire has leaked out of me. I take in a breath and open the door.

Erik's standing there with my coat in one hand and a bouquet in another—not a bouquet of flowers. A bouquet of fresh herbs.

Cilantro, basil, rosemary, thyme...

The perfect bouquet to bring to a chef.

I can't help but smile at him as he meets my eyes. "I'm sorry," he says so I can see him while he says it, and I shake my head in exasperation.

"Come on in," I tell him, and open my door wide.

CHAPTER SEVEN

ERIK

He's in a robe.

Nothing but a robe.

I don't know it for sure—he could be still wearing his underwear beneath the terrycloth. But his hair is wet, and his skin looks damp—what I can see of it—and it's clinging to the juts of his hip bones and his legs, showing off how well toned they are—

Oh, God.

Calm down. It takes everything not to crush the herbs I bought for him with my hands.

Martin invites me in and takes his coat—I stopped at a market and picked the herbs up as a peace offering. It seems to go over well. It's funny; it's a total impulse.

One minute I'm heading for the flowers, going to pull the signature, "I'm sorry and I bought you the most expensive bouquet I can find" move.

And then the next, I'm heading for the organic produce. I don't want to do the thing that gets me off the hook. I want to do the thing that makes him happy, that makes him feel seen, that makes him feel appreciated.

He puts them on his kitchen counter and while he waters them, I glance around.

His apartment is exactly how I pictured it would be— warm and cozy, eclectic but tidy. A gallery of random framed paintings and signs covers one wall of his living room. A stack of cookbooks is strewn across his dining table.

Everywhere you look, there are mismatched patterns and colorful swatches, prints of Impressionist masters and a movie poster of the film Amelie.

It's all perfect.

Perfectly Martin.

"They didn't want to shell out for a hotel room with the rest of us since you're local?" I inquire.

"No, I declined one," Martin's answer comes from down the hallway. He re-emerges from his bedroom in a pair of simple blue sweatpants paired with a white V-neck, wet patches forming on his neckline where his hair brushes his collar in long, dark copper curls. "Why stay in a sterile, uncomfortable hotel when I'm a short drive away? Even if parking on the Strip is a bitch?"

"That was more than a short drive," I argue. "That was an Uber getting lost because of all the construction, a second Uber that couldn't find your lot, and an angry power walk when I finally realized I could trust no one but myself to get me here."

This gets Martin to laugh—it's a sound I immediately want to hear more of. "True, our little city in the dessert requires a little patience right now."

Funny. I can't help but think that I need a little of his patience.

There's an awkward pause, and I dare to look down at his face. He's tiny next to me. He's washed off all the stage makeup—they applied a surprising amount of it to us for the cameras—and those perfect curls from earlier are wet waves. With his freckles and his wet hair, he looks absolutely stunning.

And I'm not thinking clearly. What I need to do is apologize, remind myself again that he's my best friend's little brother, and get the hell out of here before I run my fingers through those red curls.

Hit a point of no return.

"I really am sorry," I blurt. "I shouldn't have said that. And I didn't mean it—. You obviously know what you're doing."

Martin's lips press into a tight line, but he exhales and shakes his head. "I don't, actually. I don't know what I'm doing. But I've been so good at faking it for so long, I don't think anyone will notice the difference."

"Then keep doing what you're doing. It's obviously working."

"Is it?" Martin raises one eyebrow, smirking at me with a mischievous gleam to his eye, and my cock immediately stiffens.

I'm here in his apartment.

Alone with him, and I'm suddenly aware that this might have been exactly what he wanted all along—

Is he flirting with me? Does he want me the way that I want him?

"Want to sit?" he says quietly, his voice almost husky, and I decide to hedge my bets. He wants me to sit.

He wants me.

A framed picture of Martin's family catches my eye, right above his shoulder—he's grinning at the photographer as autumn leaves tumble down around them, and standing right next to him with that happy, dumb look on his face is his brother.

Chris.

Chris would probably hate me forever if I did anything with his brother—

And as much as I'm attracted to Martin, as much as I want to do this. Something tells me there's nothing halfway with this boy.

I'm not sure I can have what I want and keep him safe. Keep him out of the mess that I'm in.

And so, I shake my head. "It's getting late."

Martin pouts, tugging at the ends of his red curls. "I was just about to open a bottle of wine. Stay for just one glass. Then you can go."

Fuck. I'm aching to touch him—aching to press my lips against his, see if he has matching dimples anywhere else on his body,

Chris will be livid if I touch his brother, but I can restrain my desires.

Handle myself for one glass of wine.

Right?

And then tomorrow, at the Chef-Off, business as usual. Martin's just another contestant I need to defeat to get to that prize money—no matter how glorious his butt looks in his chef's whites.

Jesus. Deep breaths, Svensson.

Martin pops open a sparkling white wine and passes it to me with a lemon peel in the cup.

"I know it's trashy, but I really love my wine chilled. And with a squeeze of lemon. And all my wine glasses broke, and so now I drink out of plastic cups. Classy." He grins.

"It's perfect," I assure him, and take a sip to demonstrate. He's picked a wine that's right in between dry and sweet, and the lemon brings out citrus notes and offsets the sugar. It's masterfully balanced.

"Never apologize for plastic cups. I've had worse, trust me."

"Yeah, right." Martin curls into the corner of the couch, one cushion over from me, so we are just inches away from touching—very important inches.

It's taking every bit of restraint I have not to reach out and touch him.

"Chris has told me all about your fancy Boston restaurant, just the latest Svensson venture. Leather seats in the booths, that modern industrial look with the exposed brick and the beams in the ceiling, the expensive menus and only the freshest New England sushi."

It's all I can do not to laugh. "Oh, yeah," I say sarcastically, "my fancy restaurant that's my dream place, you bet, but has everything so tied up with investors that

I'm hoping The Chow Channel prize money buys me back a little bit of my freedom."

It comes out in one long sentence, and Martin blinks right after I say it.

I shared too much, and again, I'm ready to blame the wine—these are things I haven't said out loud to anyone, not even Chris.

But it's all true.

Somewhere along the line, I'm going to have to make a tough choice—am I a restaurant owner, or am I a master sushi cook? Do I want one great world-class restaurant on Boston's waterfront, or am I going to keep trying to build a portfolio of places globally because that's what everyone says success looks like?

Right now, at The Shark Fin and with everything else, I'm doing my best to wear both hats but it's tough to straddle all the jobs.

"So that's why you're competing in the Chef-Off," Martin surmises. "For your restaurant."

I think of Anthony, the envelope of cash, the coldness of his stare as I tried to turn down his latest investment.

"More or less," I answer.

"What will you do if you win?" Martin presses.

"I don't know."

It's an honest answer—even if I were free of the Mafia's investments in The Shark Fin, I don't know what to do with it. Press forward, go total upscale sushi, or just close the whole fucking thing and try again. "What about the Wish Café? What would you do differently?"

Martin sips his wine, deep in thought, those piercing blue eyes looking slightly tired. "Nothing," he finally says.

Moments pass, and he refills our suddenly empty wine glasses. The best of intentions always go out the window with wine and handsome men. One glass turns to two. One night turns into a lifetime.

"Nothing at all?" I push. "You wouldn't change anything on the menu? The staff?"

"I'd give it a paint job," Martin says amending his original response. "Décor and ambiance aren't really Frank's strong suit. I'd give it a good facelift—some new tables, maybe new equipment back in the kitchen, a splash of color, some plants. But other than that, no. Frank's menu is fine just the way it is."

I sit up, angling my body so I'm facing him straight on. "But don't you want to push yourself? See what you could make of it?"

Am I talking to Martin now or myself? I couldn't tell.

Martin's eyes widen, and it's clear I'm saying things to him that he's afraid to hear—but then his gaze moves down my face to my lips.

And I look back at his lips.

What will I do if he moves in to kiss me?

Hell, I want to kiss him so badly.

His lips are plump, peach, so juicy I want to bite them —but he suddenly curls up one corner of his mouth in a playful smirk.

"Can't even think about any of that until I'm staring at the ten-million-dollar check in my hands," he says, drinking from his wine cup.

"You mean my hands," I gently jab. "But I'll be sure to let you take a look at it, if that's what you want."

"Oh, I want to do more than just look at it." Martin doesn't let himself even peek at me; he pushes off the couch to get the wine bottle and refills his cup.

"No, thanks," I tell him when he tilts the bottle my way. "I'm good."

On Martin's couch, shifting back and forth between banter and serious, life-changing discussions, the scent of him wafting toward me, mingling with the sharpness of those new herbs, smelling delicious. Hour pass, and those two glasses of wine become five.

Again, the best of intentions and all that. Oh well. There's nowhere else I'd rather be.

Eventually drowsy, I rest my head back against the couch, trying not to fall asleep with a smile on my face, the wine making my thoughts—my dreams?—heavy and sweet.

Dreams of Martin.

My phone buzzes, bright and early.

I peel open my eyes, confused. Where am I?

A poster of Amelie stares at me from the corner of the wall, and I remember with a jolt.

I'm in Martin's apartment.

I came here last night—did something happen? I'm still in my clothes, so I don't think we did anything.

I know that I wanted to last night.

I still want it. In fact, just the thought is enough to take me from slight morning wood to full on "you're next to a gorgeous ginger god, idiot, let's do this" hard-on.

But I sit up and find him asleep on the couch next to me, the finished bottle of wine tipped over on the floor.

It's almost seven.

My alarms were set for three times—the first, six-thirty, when I needed to get up. Then at six-forty, for after I ignored the first alarm.

And this last alarm was for six forty-five, for when I really needed to get my ass moving so I wasn't late for the second round of the competition—

And we slept through all of them.

Martin leans to one side, his hair sprawled out on the cushion above him, those natural spiral curls already formed. His dimple is visible, since he's kind of smiling in his sleep, and he looks so peaceful, I hate to wake him.

But I have to.

Otherwise, we'll miss the second round of the competition, and neither of us will get to hold that big money check at the end of the Chef-Off.

"Martin," I whisper, tenderly touching his shoulder. A shiver goes down my spine when I make contact with his bare skin, but I resist the urge to start something and let him wake up.

"Erik?" he murmurs, stretching, and his eyes go wide as saucers. "Holy fuck, what happened?"

"Nothing," I assure him, taking a step back so he can have his space. "Nothing happened—I woke up with all my clothes on, and so did you."

Martin rubs his eyes and then glares at me, "I meant what happened, like why are you here at my apartment? Not... you know..."

"Oh, right." The scene of the crime seems pretty obvious to me—we drank a little too much wine, got a little too relaxed while we chatted on the couch, and fell asleep.

Martin nods, standing up—his bedhead is a sunburst of snarls, a lion's mane around his face, and it's so adorable, I almost can't stand it.

But now's not the time to comment on such things.

We've got to get back down to the Strip for the next challenge in the competition.

"Listen," I say, "I'm going to get a head start and go change at my hotel. I'll meet you at the challenge?"

Martin nods his head and just before I walk out his door, he says in a morning-soft whisper, "Thank you for the herbs."

I catch his eye and smile. "Anytime."

The elevator takes forever, so I jog down the stairs, surprisingly cheerful despite my rushed start to my day. I didn't fuck Martin; I didn't even kiss him. Both things I'm still desperate to do, and every time I talk to him, it's more and more apparent that the two of us are well-matched—but I shared a meal with him, spent the night deep in conversation, and got to see his apartment.

I'd spent the night with him, even if it was the two of us sprawled on the couch, fully dressed.

It isn't what I ultimately hoped for—but it's something.

I'm so stupidly joyful as I come down the stairs, I almost don't notice another person coming up—and when I crash into him, a familiar face wrinkles in confusion. "Erik?"

It's Chris.

Fuck. That office job sends him on the road, and he once mentioned something about crashing with Martin when he's in Vegas on business. What awful timing.

My stomach tangles with nerves. "Hey, man," I say fast —how the fuck am I going to explain this? Skipping down the stairs after spending the night at his brother's?

"What are you... Oh, no. No fucking way." Chris seems to have figured it out himself. Or at least he thinks he has.

"It's not what it looks like." I hold up my hands in case he wants to throw punches. "Honestly. I just brought a coat to your brother and fell asleep on his couch."

"Right," Chris intones, his jaw set with anger. "And did you steal his coat, so you'd have to return it? Was that your big plan? Was that the whole reason you got into this competition in the first place? So you could nail Martin?"

Anger hits me. I get why he's protective of his brother. Hell, they'd been all the other had for so long and Martin was still so young.

But he knows me better than that – and he's the one that fucking suggested I do the competition in the first place.

I didn't even know Martin was competing.

That's probably not the biggest consideration from his point of view at the moment, though.

"Chris, no. Listen. The two of us grabbed dinner after the challenge today—he made it to the top three, can you believe it?" I say. "And then he left his coat at the restaurant, so I brought it to him, and I fell asleep on his couch after some wine. That's it. I swear."

I wait, unsure if he's about to drive a fist through my jaw. Seriously hoping not, because that's going to be a rough sell on nation TV.

Chris loosens up, slumping down, then slugs my arm hard. "That's for making me think that you banged my brother," he says.

His voice takes on a serious note. "Because, Erik, you remember you're involved in the Mafia, right? You haven't forgotten about that?"

"I'm not *involved in the Mafia*. They've got a chokehold on my business. Totally different things." But even as I say it, I know he's right.

I can't get involved with Martin. Not when I could endanger him by exposing him to someone like Anthony.

Anthony Napali is a scary fucking dude—and until I am completely clear of him in my life, I can't drag Martin into it. Or anyone, for that matter. I can't.

"You're right. Things are way too dangerous right now. I'll back off."

"Good." Chris checks his watch. "Now, you'd better run. Hard to get a rideshare this time of day. Don't let me catch you at my brother's place again until you have your pest control problem taken care of."

I'm so busy dashing to catch my Uber, I don't put it together at first—

But it sounds like Chris's only problem with me and Martin is that I have a potentially unsafe situation brewing at my restaurant.

It sounds like, if I take care of the Mafia issues, he'll be fine with me and Martin.

It sounds like I might even be lucky enough to get his blessing.

CHAPTER EIGHT

MARTIN

Another challenge down.

This time, we have to make our very best sandwiches—another tricky task.

On the surface, it seems like a pedestrian challenge, something that just anyone could do. But there was so much to consider—the meat selection, vegetables for the right amount of crunch, sauces...the 'aesthetic' of it all...

I panic just thinking about all the choices, and in the pantry, I freeze.

But I glance over at Erik who loads his basket with ingredients—roasted red peppers, mustard, apricots, an entire Cornish hen, and then I remember something Frank likes to say.

"A sandwich is only as good as the bread it's on."

I grab a crusty loaf of nine-grain bread, some fresh mozzarella, and the ingredients to make herby green goddess dressing with tarragon and lemon. Cucumbers, radishes, and avocado will give a nice crunch.

I pickle the radishes, mash the avocado with salt and pepper, and wrap my tall, messy sandwich with paper to serve it for the judges.

"Looks amazing," Erik compliments me as I bring it up to the front, and I sneak a peek at his offering, shocked by his invention.

He's made his own jam with the roasted red peppers and the apricot, and paired it with the chicken, caramelized onions and a garlic paste on a baguette. From the judge's first bite of Erik's sandwich, it's mouth-watering.

I'm not surprised when he makes it through this round, landing in the top three yet again—and I try not to be shocked when I, too, stand up there in the top three.

Five contestants are let go.

Only five of us left, now, and two more days of the competition.

The judges will whittle it down to three tomorrow, then two on Thursday—and then we've got Friday off to rest before we face off for the finals.

I stop myself, shaking my head as I change out of my chef's whites and into street clothes.

I've got to keep assuming it's going to be Erik and me in the end.

It'll be Erik—that sandwich he just served up was stunning enough to be on any fine restaurant's menu.

But once again, I'm having a hard time believing I'll still be here on Sunday.

"Hey," I call to Erik as I exit the conference center and come down the concrete steps. He's standing there in jeans and a sweater, his long hair tied back, his Viking blue eyes the same color as the cool spring sky. "Nice work in there."

"You too." He's trying very hard to keep his distance, even though I'm giving him the most flirtatious poses I have.

We woke up next to each other on the couch, and while I'd been relieved that nothing had happened—I wouldn't want to get together with Erik when I was drunk—another part of me was disappointed.

But judging by the way Erik is avoiding my gaze, I'm the only one.

"I didn't get to finish my sandwich," I say. "Do you want to go find something to eat? More sushi? Pasta? Hot dog stand?"

Shut up, I chide myself, *you're trying way too hard.*

But I can't help it. I'm overwhelmed with desire, especially after seeing him all snoozy on my couch this morning—last night in the bath, I'd revved myself up and I hadn't yet gotten to kiss him.

But Erik purses his lips and gives his head a quick shake. "Sorry, I'm a little hungover and I've got no appetite. Plus I've actually got some things I need to take care of. But I'll see you at tomorrow's challenge."

Before I can ask him why, exactly, he's changed his mind when last night, he was eye-fucking me every chance he had, Erik takes off toward his toward the hotel.

"He's cute." Another competitor, a tough-looking woman named Lettie who made it into the top three with Erik and me today, comes over to me.

She's scrappy, her black hair cut in an asymmetrical bob and tattoos covering her arms and chest. She nudges me like we've been friends forever. "I'm starving. Want to get something to eat?"

I almost tell her no, because wherever I go, I'll be dining with the humiliation of Erik's rejection hanging over my head. But then my stomach rumbles with hunger, giving me away.

Lettie grins. "I know just the place. You eat meat?"

"Habitually," I tell her.

"Great. You'll love it. Let's go."

Lettie's restaurant of choice is a surprisingly well-lit biker bar just right off-Strip, the walls plastered not with paint or wallpaper, but bumper stickers. It's an open kitchen, and all the men handling the grills are bearded Harley Davidson-types, who wave cheerfully at Lettie as soon as we get to the register.

"My cousins," she explains. "We'll take a five-meat platter. Double brisket, double pulled pork, and a spicy chicken. Also, two orders of coleslaw, sweet potato fries, and honey biscuits. You want wings? They've got wings."

This question is directed to me, but I'm already so bewildered by the sheer amount of food she's just ordered, I shake my head.

"Put it on my tab." Lettie grabs a couple of beers from the cooler, then leads us to a table that overlooks the sidewalk.

"How is it?" Lettie asks a few minutes later after our food's arrived and I've gotten my first bites.

I'm too busy chewing to answer—but it's all the best barbeque I've ever eaten. "Is this where you work?"

Lettie shakes her head, scrunching her nose. "Naw. They won't share the grill with me, even though I can run circles around them. I'm up doing line work at one of the casino places. Candlelight Lounge. Do you know it?"

I do.

"The owner has his head up his ass, but it's decent money and he lets me handle dessert." Lettie pauses to swig her beer. "What about you?"

I tell her about the Wish Café, about Frank McIntosh, and her eyes widen. "You're working with Frank?" She shakes her head in shock. "No wonder you're hitting that top three twice in a row."

I chuckle. "That's been pure luck, I assure you."

"No way." Lettie tosses a piece of brisket in her mouth. "You're the real deal. Same with that hot Viking. What's his story? You guys seem chummy."

My pulse spikes at the thought of Erik. So, others have noticed there's something between us—I don't know whether to be embarrassed or glad that others see me stake my claim.

"He's my older brother's best friend," I explain.

"I don't mean to pry," Lettie continues, munching a French fry, "but you guys are..."

"Gay?" I laugh.

"So are you two an item or what?"

I sigh. "I wish," I admit, gazing at the bumper stickers on the wall.

Lettie raises one eyebrow. "So it's a crush, huh? How very high school."

"Well, to be fair, I was in junior high school when I met Erik. At that age, though, I thought I had a chance with a guy like him," I say defensively.

Lettie snickers. "He likes you. Trust me. I've seen the way he looks at you—he lights up when you talk to him. Plus, he can't keep his eyes off your ass."

"Really?"

"Sure," Lettie says. "It's a great ass."

I'm so busy preening over this compliment and that she thinks Erik likes me, I almost don't see him at first.

But movement out the window catches my eye.

A man, standing outside a street food cart, eating a falafel wrap, his hair blowing slightly in the breeze.

Erik.

My heart sinks into my stomach.

Not hungry, huh? There he is, scarfing down his wrap like he hasn't eaten in weeks.

So it wasn't that he didn't want to eat.

It was that he didn't want to eat with me.

I set down my fork.

Suddenly, I'm the one who isn't hungry.

Lettie's notices I'm not paying attention to her.

She follows my sightline outside, and I'm about to explain to her the situation with Erik when we both pause.

A long black limo pulls up to the curb near the falafel cart, and a man with greasy black hair in a suit gets out, straightening his tie.

He spots Erik, walks over to him with his hand extended.

Erik looks a little surprised but shakes the man's hand with recognition. The man gestures to a fancy place across the street and Erik nods.

Then the two of them walk off and the limo pulls away.

"Weird," I say, frowning. "I wonder if Erik knows that guy." It's a stupid question. Clearly Erik knows him. I wonder where from and where they're headed off to.

But Lettie has a strange expression on her face.

"You'd better hope he doesn't," she finally says. "That guy's bad news."

"What do you mean?"

"I mean," Lettie says, grabbing one of the fries and popping it in her mouth, "that guy is in the mob. And guys like that only have two kinds of acquaintances—accomplices or future victims."

My blood runs cold. "Are you sure? How can you tell?"

"I can tell." She's tracing one of her tattoos, a delicate Christian cross that points up her forearm. "Trust me. I grew up in a neighborhood full of guys just like that."

Suddenly, it's hard to breathe.

Mafia. The second she says it, I know she's right. I grew up in New York. And it's not like Vegas doesn't have its share of connected families.

And Erik just shook his hand.

"He's definitely not one of them," I tell Lettie. "Look at him—look at his hair. Look at his smile. You think they'd let a guy like this into the Mafia?"

Come on. A Swedish chef with a penchant for fish in the mob? That's a little far fetched.

Even for weird shit going down in Vegas.

Lettie tilts her head. "Then Erik's in big trouble. That guy looked mean. You see his shoes? No creases at all. That means he's not the one who carries out the orders; he's the one who gives them."

I process what Lettie is suggesting—Erik has a hit on him? He's got the Mafia breathing down his neck about something? I wish I could ask Chris. But there's no time for that.

"Come on," I say, grabbing one more honey biscuit. "We've got to see what's going on. Erik might need our help."

CHAPTER NINE

ERIK

I couldn't do it.

When Martin asked me to get food with him again, I wanted to say yes.

I want to say yes to everything he could possibly ask from me—but I can't stop thinking about what Chris said.

At least one investor of The Shark Fin has Mafia ties—and Anthony's rap sheet shows me he's not the kind of guy you mess with.

Right now, this is between him and me.

I don't want to give him any ideas there's anyone else connected to me, anyone he could use for leverage.

The last thing I want to do is get Martin involved in anything dangerous. Even though I didn't want to say no, I didn't have a choice.

I'll keep him as far from me as possible, so Anthony can't somehow slither in and get his hands on him. Martin can't be a part of this.

Which means he can't be a part of my life.

Not until I take care of things with Anthony.

Still, when I hit a falafel place down the street, I'm barely paying attention to how it tastes. I can only think about Martin.

How he looked today during the challenge, bending over his countertop, concentrating hard, making sure every detail was perfect.

And it had been—the dish he presented to the judges was phenomenal, smart and fresh.

The kind of meal you want to eat again and again.

He's everything I want and more: gorgeous, funny and sharp as a tack. Hell, he's got the most incredible body I've ever seen.

A body that would make a monk cry.

I'm fantasizing about having Martin in Boston to celebrate the day after I win the cash prize, and I'm trying to decide whether he looks sexiest from the front or from the back when a limo pulls up to the curb beside me.

"Erik? I thought that was you."

Familiar voice. A little smarmy. Anthony Napali, in the flesh, standing next to this falafel cart.

"Anthony." I try to keep the tension in my voice down. "What are you doing here?"

What the fuck is this guy doing in Vegas? Of course, I have a hunch and it's not good news for me.

"This is where the competition is, isn't it?" Anthony juts his chin toward the Las Vegas Strip and the casino with huge letters on the marquee: *Chow Channel Chef-Off Competition – All This Week*.

"Sounds like a good time. Came to watch the proceedings."

"You came all this way to watch me cook? You can see that any day in Boston." I go for light, though my voice sounds tight.

Is this Anthony's idea of a threat? Has he found out that I know who he is? Does he know I plan on buying out his investment, thus cutting off his lucrative money-laundering haven?

"Don't get such a big head." Anthony reaches up and pats my cheek like I'm his grandson; I fight not to recoil. "I came to watch all the contestants, not just you."

He leans over to wink at me as we reach the steps of the casino. "Sometimes, it helps to have friends in high places."

I want to let him walk up the stairs alone, but he pauses, waiting for me to go with him. And as we march up, back into the events center, I wonder if I'm marching toward my doom.

"You say you have a friend here?" I'm pretty sure the best policy when you're being targeted by a member of the Mafia is to just keep quiet. I need to know what I'm dealing with here.

"That I do," Anthony answers as we come through the doors. The conference center lights are already off, but Anthony leads into the main hall—where the Chow Channel's filming—like he knows the place inside and out. "A very old friend who, I happen to believe, has the very best seat in the house—aha!"

We're back in the giant temporary kitchen. Everything's been reset for tomorrow's challenge. I expect producers and the camera operators to be lingering, but the room is empty except for one person.

"Hiroko!" Anthony extends his arms to one of the judges and the two of them embrace. "How are you? Older than the last time I saw you."

"Yes, well," Hiroko responds good-naturedly. "Time hasn't been kind to you, either, my friend. These are new."

He gestures to the crows' feet wrinkles lining Anthony's eyes, and Anthony cackles, glancing back at me to gauge my reaction.

"Hiroko and I go way back, don't we, old friend?" Anthony explains. "He told me if I was ever in town, I should look him up for a drink. Here I am."

"Here you are," Hiroko agrees, his mood indiscernible. "But I told Anthony that I am busy with the competition, and I told him to come watch instead."

Anthony really does have an old friend to get him in the door. Fuck. Time to ratchet my pulse down, now I know I'm not going to be stuffed into a body bag and thrown into Lake Mead with cement boots on my feet.

But wait.

Maybe Hiroko is some sort of Japanese mobster, part of the Yakuza. Does the terrifying Japanese crime syndicate have alliances with Boston's Italian mob? Maybe this is the moment when Anthony hands me off so Hiroko can properly punish me with his sushi knives.

"How do you know each other?" Hiroko asks, pointing at the two of us, and Anthony glances at me with a strange look on his face.

"Kind of a funny story, isn't it, Erik?" he says.

"Not really," I rush to say. "I own a restaurant in Boston. Anthony's one of my investors." I'm about to say something else when Anthony's eye catches something behind me.

Two silhouettes in the open door, staring into the kitchen.

"Who's there?" Anthony's voice is pure menace. My first real glimpse of what he must be like when he's in full Mafia mode.

Pretty terrifying shit.

"Hey," comes a shaky boyish voice, one I instantly recognize.

Martin moves forward into the lights, accompanied by one of the women in our competition, the one with tattoos and the cool haircut. "Sorry, we were just getting ready to leave and thought we heard voices."

He flashes me a worried glance. He fucking came here to rescue me.

Tiny little redheaded Martin, with his freckles and his downhome cooking and his big heart. And more balls than most guys I know, which includes some real tough guys.

Somehow, he's figured it out.

He's pieced together that I have a little mob problem in my life right now—and right now, more than ever, I wish I could kiss him.

Kiss him for sticking around and keeping an eye on me, even though I've been a jerk.

"You sure did." Anthony faces Martin, the smile on his face one I haven't seen before. Mocking, predatory. "I'm Anthony, and you are?"

He reaches out for Martin's hand and holds it just a little too long, and a bubble of rage fills my chest.

"Martin." He locks eyes with me until Anthony lets go of his hand, letting me know he's all right, and that Anthony's no threat to me—but I'm not sure if Martin understands just how close we are to danger.

"And this is Lettie." Lettie doesn't let Anthony touch her; she stands at a distance, her jaw tight, her lips in a thin line.

"That's what they're naming angels these days, is it?" Anthony trills, and I can't stop rolling my eyes. It's a cheap, overused line—but he says it with a weird bravado that tells me occasionally, it works. One look at his ritzy suit and his power stance, and some people probably melt like butter.

"You in the restaurant business too, eh? You two kids got any plans for dinner later? I might have some work for you." Anthony steps even closer to Martin. This time, Martin's gaze is frantic. He needs help.

Now it's my turn.

I step between Martin and Anthony, wrapping an arm around him. There's absolutely nothing I wouldn't do to protect this boy.

Keep him safe.

"Actually, baby boy, you okay with eating in tonight? It's been such a long day, and I just want to order pizza and crash."

My trick works.

Anthony leans back, his eyebrows furrowed. "Whoa, Erik, you two have some kinda thing going on?"

Martin kisses my cheek.

"Going on two years now," he says brightly, and I try to ignore the parts of me that grow hard at the very thought.

If two years from now, Martin and I were able to say that about each other, I'd be a happy man.

But for now, it looks like this is enough to make Anthony back off Martin. Initially, I'd planned to keep him out of this entirely. Since that's not possible, I'm clearly staking a claim.

Stay away from Martin or answer to me.

He pats my back and says, "Have a fun night, kids. Rest up. Competition's tomorrow, bright and early. Come on, Hiroko. You owe me a drink."

Everyone can breathe after that.

Lettie, Martin, and I walk back out of the casino just in time for the setting sun casting a golden light across the gaudy yet strangely beautiful silhouette of downtown Las Vegas.

"How'd you know where I went?" I ask.

Lettie nods at a restaurant across the street. "We saw you talking to him from R&R's," she explains. "Looked like he strong-armed you across the street?"

"No," I correct. "He just asked me to walk with him, and I did."

Both Lettie and Martin scrunch up their faces in concern, and I sigh.

Enough trying to hide this shit.

I might not want to drag Martin into this, but clearly, keeping him in the dark isn't working. Maybe if I'm honest, he'll listen to me and stay out of the crosshairs.

So, I explain everything—how I opened my restaurant in Boston a few years back and had some too-eager investors right from the start. I tell them about the phone call from Benny, how Anthony has been pushing more and more money at me, how I'm concerned he knows I've discovered his ties to the mob.

"So that's why you're here," Martin says, his voice sounding tired. "You're going to use the cash prize to buy out his share of the investments."

"Assuming I can even make it that far," I say. "There's a lot riding on this Chef-Off. For all of us."

Lettie says her goodbyes, telling me to sleep with one eye open—I haven't asked her yet how she figured out that Anthony was a gangster, but her tattoos tell enough of the story for me to piece it together.

And I've heard of the guys who run R&R—they're a tough crowd, too. Not as scary as the mob, but you don't want to get on their bad side, or so say some friends of mine connected to the Sin City culinary scene.

She hugs Martin, then it's just the two of us standing on the curb, a new level of honesty unlocked between us.

And I'm about to take it even further.

Fuck it. Time to show your hand, or whatever metaphor works in this Vegas context.

"I've got to tell you," I say, "I ran into Chris this morning in your stairwell. He... was not very happy that I'd spent the night in your apartment."

"I know," Martin answers. He hands me his phone, scrolling angry texts from his brother, telling him to stay away from his best friend.

"But I also told him to go to hell. I'll always be his little brother, but I'm an adult and I make my own decisions." He glances back up at me; there's something radiating from his blue eyes—a bit of daring, a bit of hope.

"Does that mean you still want to eat in tonight?" I say, suddenly nervous in a way I haven't been in a very long time, maybe ever, with a prospective date. "My hotel's right there."

"Great idea." Martin puts his hand in mine again, and I nearly lose it right there on the pavement. "Pizza?"

"Pizza," I agree, and hope to God that pizza is actually code for something else.

Because while I am getting hungry for dinner, I'm even hungrier for the chance to finally kiss him and hold him and fuck him, and I'm crossing my fingers he feels the same way.

CHAPTER TEN

MARTIN

P izza.

It arrives within fifteen minutes, just long enough for the cheap beer I'd guzzled at R&R Barbeque with Lettie to leave my system.

We spend a few minutes making small talk about the day's competition, predicting what will happen tomorrow.

Basically, we're dancing all around it.

Eventually, I reach across Erik to get to the pizza. My arm grazes his abs – how a chef manages to keep six-pack abs is a question that's going need considerable explanation, I decide—and I let my hand linger just long enough.

Long enough to feel his interest stirring. Long enough for his eyes to cut to my face.

The desire in the air is so strong, it's palpable.

But Erik's restraining himself. Always the gentleman, always waiting to make sure—very sure—I'm on board.

And finally, when I can't take it any longer, I toss my half-eaten slice back into the box and spring on him.

His kiss tastes spicy at first, the remnants of the marinara and the pepperoni lingering. The more we kiss, the more I'm able to taste him, Erik, the Viking, and my skin tingles with shivers—everywhere.

His lips against mine are warm, his kiss sizzling but slow. He's taking his time. Savoring. This is a man who knows what he's doing and is willing to take the time to do things right.

The promise of that pulls a groan from my lips.

I can't remember the last time I was kissed like this, like I'm something precious. His hands cradle both sides of my face, holding me steady, and I open my mouth just slightly, repositioning my own lips on his.

Erik groans and his tongue tangles with my own.

His beard is surprisingly soft—when it presses against my neck, it doesn't tickle or scratch. I couldn't grow a beard like that in a million years.

My hands run over his shoulders, feeling thick biceps beneath his flannel shirt, and I find his buttons, undoing them one at a time. God, he's so fucking hot.

Erik pulls back suddenly, searching my face. "Are you sure it's right to do this?"

I frown, fighting through the fog of my desire. "Why, is there some sort of rule about contestants sleeping together?"

"No." Erik shakes his head with a rueful smile. "I meant, are you sure this is something you want to do, really want to do? Martin—I don't just want to fuck you once. I want to…"

He can't even finish his sentence; he leans back over me with an almost primal growl, running his hand down my chest, wrapping his strong fingers around my waist.

"I want you, too," I whisper, and then he's yanking off my shirt, exposing my chest to the cool air conditioned room.

Heat's building in my body as his mouth trails down my neck, past my collarbone, kissing the spot right in the middle of my chest. My whole body erupts in chills.

Fire and ice: that's what it's like being with this Viking in the middle of the desert.

When he takes one of my nipples in his mouth, I arch my back, groaning—it feels so fucking good, and I'm already rock hard. My hand slips through his hair, tugging on it slightly, so he'll know I'm up for a bit of rough, dirty fun.

With an almost guttural sound, he obliges and bites me lightly on my nipple.

I can't stand it any longer, the need to feel him. Reaching down, I find his pants and unbutton them, tugging them down, and...

Oh, God. There it is.

It has to be eight inches long, so thick—big enough to fill me up and then some.

Erik's eyes darken with lust as he slides off my own pants. He looks at me and runs a finger along my stiff member.

"You're gorgeous," he says, his voice rough with desire. He moves as if to go down on me, and while I can't wait to experience that, right now I want nothing more than to just feel that stiff cock inside me.

I need him.

I need him now.

"Fuck me," I whisper.

Erik pulls a condom, tears the foil, rolls it on himself. His cock is perfect—long and thick, twitching with desire as he lubes it up. I spread my legs, positioning my ass on the edge of his bed—which we somehow made it to, in the midst of that lustful haze—and I ready myself for it.

Everything stills, and he's positioned there above me just looking down at me. Something flickers in his eyes, a kind of wanting that's not lust. Desire that's deeper than sex. A rawness that's totally unexpected.

My heart's beating—with anticipation and with the nascent feeling of something else. A richer deeper feeling I'm afraid to name.

But Erik's not afraid. He holds my eye and slowly thrusts into me, several smooth moves that fill me up and stretch me. I cry out, I can't help it, and he captures my lips with his.

I can hardly stand it—it's so hot, and he feels so good, and after all these years of fantasizing about this very moment, it's happening. He's so big.

I lean into him and kiss him, wrapping my legs around his. One hand finds my chest, teasing my nipple. He slides in and out with a practiced control that promises to take me to the edge and tip me over, into sweet agony.

"This is so good," I moan against his lip. "Keep fucking me. Just like that."

The beginnings of an orgasm throb in the base of my spine. I'm lightheaded, dizzy, spinning toward a finish—

And then Erik wraps a hand around my cock, stroking it soft and gently, and it happens.

I whimper and my whole body quivers as an orgasm floods through me. My toes curl, my cry almost primitive.

My brain goes completely blank.

He pounds into me for long minutes until I'm raw from crying out his name in an endless spiral of pleasure. Just before he reaches his own climax, he puts a hand under my chin and tenderly tilts my mouth to his. His kiss is interrupted by a long, lusty moan, and then he too is spent. His orgasm is everlasting, but when it finally ends, he tugs me down to the carpet, and we lie there for a minute, legs intertwined.

His hand finds mine, lacing our fingers together.

"Hi," he whispers.

"Hi," I whisper back.

"So… Saturday." There's a hint of something in Erik's voice, but I can't quite detect what it is. I turn to look at him but he's staring up at the ceiling, deep in thought.

"Saturday." As soon as I say it, I realize what he means.

Saturday. We're the last two in the Chef-Off competition, and on Saturday, we'll no longer be just Erik and Martin, two people who've been flirting with each other for years.

Two people who just sated each other with pleasure.

Two people who just hinted at the possibilities beyond this.

We'll be the final two.

And only one of us will win.

"But first, tomorrow." Erik turns on his side, propping up his head with one hand. "Do you have any plans?"

"We're off tomorrow," I say. "Nothing yet." I trace circles on his muscular chest, already wishing I had time to explore his body again.

"Want to come to Boston? I need to check on the restaurant." He pauses before finishing with, "I need to make sure Anthony hasn't turned it into a full-on Mafia speakeasy while I've been gone."

I think it's a few-hours flight each way. But those are hours I can spend with Erik.

"Yes. I would love to see your restaurant."

CHAPTER ELEVEN

ERIK

I shouldn't be nervous, but I am.

For multiple reasons.

First, I'm nervous to come back to The Shark Fin—especially after my encounter with Anthony in Vegas. Hopefully he wasn't offended I took Martin out from under his nose. Part of me knows this is ridiculous—he needs the restaurant to be open and functional so he can keep using it to launder his dirty money. He's not going to burn it down.

But I'm also nervous it's finally happening.

Me and Martin.

Last night was the best night of my life—the two of us together, and we would have spent the whole night together, sleeping in each other's arms, but he wanted to get back to his apartment, so he was all showered and ready for tomorrow.

"You sure you'll be all right getting home?" I'd asked him a dozen times, and he kept grinning up at me, that dimple popping into the corner of his mouth.

"I can handle myself just fine."

That was the truest statement I'd ever heard—he'd handled things with Anthony brilliantly, following my lead as I pretended he and I were together, and last night...

He'd handled things last night just fine. Better than fine.

Especially the second time. And the third.

But now I'm showing him my restaurant.

The business I started from scratch, the receptacle of all my hopes and dreams—and I hope he'll like it.

Or, at least, see its potential. It's true I have a couple of other restaurants in nearby cities, a bistro in Portland Maine and sushi restaurants in Portsmouth and Providence. But the Shark Fin: that's where my heart is.

Maybe if he sees it, he'll see why I'm going through all this trouble with the Chef-Off competition, why I want to save it from dirty Mafia money.

We take the earliest flight out, and he sleeps for most of it, his head resting on my shoulder. When he wakes up and asks for a blanket, he spreads it over us both.

At first, I think he's just being thoughtful and something about the tender move has my heart beating a little faster. Then the real fun starts when I feel his fingers slide across the plane of my stomach and under the waistband of my jeans.

My eyes cut in his direction, but his eyes are closed.

Innocent, asleep, just resting a hand in my lap.

Thank God the seats next to me and across the aisle are vacant. The cabin lights are low. Any passengers nearby are rows away and I haven't seen a flight attendant in hours.

His hand expertly wraps around the head of my cock, stroking, stroking. But leisurely, slowly, as though he's got a whole fucking flight to torture me. Minutes, long minutes, pass. Pleasure builds steadily but doesn't crest, my cock so hard it's straining to be free and my balls heavy with desire.

A flight attendant walks by, glances our way, keeps going.

Martin's hand falls away, and then back, closes back around my shaft and head. Stroking, stroking, even slower now.

Sweet fucking agony.

It's taking everything I've got to stay quiet, and when I give a desperate little thrust into his hand—what is he reducing me to?—he slides it away.

He gives his head a shake. His eyes say, *did I say you could come? Bad boy.*

Holy Christ.

My cock is iron, and I want to take him here. Spread his legs, hook his ankles over the empty seats in front of us, and plunge into him until his throat is raw from screaming my name. Take that, TSA. Whatever look I give him makes him giggle, then he winks, nibbling at his lip until a full-bodied ripple of desire racks my body.

The effect she's having on me is unbelievable.

Finally, he glances around, and then slides his hand back inside my pants. This time, he's pumping with purpose and I'm almost there, right there, so close. I've been crossing the desert for days and an oasis is in sight...When he stops.

Just stops.

I'm practically blind with lust, literally panting.

This tiny creature, this wicked brat, is reducing me to pure lust. Taking me to the edge, then denying me what I want, in a place where I'm powerless to do anything.

Just the thought has me primal.

Suddenly, there's an announcement. *Prepare for landing. We've arrived in Boston.*

He gives me a wink, and somehow, just when I manage to calm things down, he gets me. A brush of the hand under the blanket over my cock. Leaning forward to toss a napkin into the passing flight attendants' waste bag and he's grazing my nipple again, accidentally on purpose... Dragging his nails up my leg with a demure dip of the eyes and a whispered, "Sorry, nervous flier."

The plane touches down, and we're out of the airport and in my SUV in minutes.

I'm hardly able to speak—and driving safely is definitely questionable—but I know where I'm headed.

Early Spring in Boston. Thankfully warm.

Five minutes outside Logan and we're pulling into a completely empty parking lot. It's a trailhead I like to hike sometimes. Even though it's in the middle of the city, it's a green, wild feel. And it's almost always vacant.

Just like it is this morning.

I'm out of the car, and around to the other side, opening his door.

"What—"

I don't let him finish. I somehow manage to kiss him, demanding, almost angry. Have you ever been fucking tortured for hours?

Me neither, until now.

His seatbelt unhooked, I swing him up and kick the door shut behind me, heading up the trail with determined strides. Sometimes it's fucking great to be six-four and muscled for raiding distant countries.

His eyes are on my face, looking a little nervous. We get maybe five hundred yards up the trail when I swing off the path, muscling our way into the trees. Just ahead, I see a huge boulder with a ledge. The area's totally private, and I intend to make great fucking use of this.

"Martin?" My voice is a growl. But it's also a question.

I've never prayed so hard for a yes.

His hands move to my belt, and he falls to his knees.

Holy Jesus.

My pants and boxers are down, my cock free and he's wrapping those amazing lips around it. Sucking the tip, practically taking me the whole way into his throat. God, some relief from the tension.

Basically, I'm a puppet on this boy's string. His hand grasps the base of my shaft, and I fist my hand into his hair even as I'm begging him to stop.

I want to do this a hundred times. A thousand times. But that's not what I want right now.

What I want is him. To be inside him.

To give as good as I've gotten for the last three hours.

He stands up and kisses me, and—holy shit—it's the hottest thing I can imagine.

I point to his jeans. "Off," I manage through gritted teeth.

And he obliges, again holding eye contact and sliding them down. Inch by inch. I can hardly think straight.

I lift him up, balancing him on the ledge of the rock and my cock finds his hot center. Plunges into the hot, tight piece of heaven. He's hard and he's ready and, *God.*

His legs wrap around me, pulling me close, pulling me deeper.

Possessive. Claiming.

My hips move on their own accord, like they've done this a thousand times and will a thousand more. My peace. My destiny. My world. I don't know where I end and where he begins. There's nothing I want more than to be even deeper inside him.

The only way to get there is to keep pushing inside him. Thrusting, Driving. Claiming.

Over and over, the sound of his moans urges me on.

Mine. Mine. Mine.

His hands have slid under my shirt, and his nails drag down my back. The exquisite pain drives me deeper inside him and he screams my name. And I'm lost.

Coming. Jolt after jolt after jolt. Twitching deep inside him.

Mine. Mine. He's mine. All mine.

Jesus.

I don't move for a long time, my head just resting on his. Staying inside him.

Mine.

He looks up and gives me a slightly shy, wicked grin.

Tries to speak. He has to clear his throat, and then says, "So, Boston?"

Boston, indeed.

W e finally pull up to my restaurant, I put the car in park and turn in the seat.

"I don't know what state it's in," I warn him, "since I've been gone this past week. It might be a disaster."

"I promise I'll look past any initial flaws I see," Martin says, and leans forward to kiss me on the nose before he gets out of the car.

With a deep, bracing breath, I take him inside.

It's not bad.

I can see a few tables that need to be bussed, but other than that, everything's in operating order.

It's a restaurant to be proud of.

I show Martin around, letting him take stock of the bar that I had specially made out of recycled wood from Peru. I let him see the kitchen, our set-up, all of it.

Martin doesn't let go of my hand once, and he takes in everything I tell him, asking questions occasionally.

"I can see why the Mafia chose your operation," he says at the end of the tour. "It's the perfect location—central to three main streets, right across the street from the park, and the back door opens up to the alley."

"Great, I've been chosen by the Mafia," I say drily. "I'm so lucky."

Martin giggles, and I take him with me to chat with the head server, Tom, who is in charge of the dining room today for lunch.

"Everything's fine," he confirms when I ask how things have been going this week in my absence, "but Manny had to go home sick, so we're down a line cook. We were a little backed up for a while, but Gretchen managed to get us back on track. All the orders are out except for his."

Tom gestures to an old man in a Hawaiian shirt, sitting in the corner booth, sipping a drink. "He's been here since opening and hasn't ordered any food. Just nursing a drink and staring out the window."

"Maybe he's waiting for someone," Martin points out.

"Maybe," I echo, but my mind immediately goes elsewhere—do members of the Mafia ever wear Hawaiian shirts?

As if he can tell we're talking about him, the old man suddenly arches around, making eye contact with Tom, who rushes to the table and gets his order.

"He wants something off-menu," Tom reports.

"What's he asking for?"

"Puttanesca." Tom shrugs, looking at me. "I told him I'd ask."

"I'll make it," Martin instantly says. "I'd love to make something in your kitchen."

There's something about the idea of him cooking in my kitchen that has me hard all over again.

"You would deprive a hungry old man a full plate of pasta?" Martin snorts, tying an apron over his T-shirt. My eyes take his impossibly slender waist beneath that shirt, and all of a sudden, I'm back in the woods, buried inside him, hearing angels sing.

"Absolutely," I tell him. "For the integrity of the brand. The Shark Fin, don't forget."

"I think the brand should just be 'good fucking food,'" he says, grinning.

Ten minutes later, Martin's got a gorgeous square plate with three spirals of thick, mouthwatering homemade pasta in marinara sauce, capers and green olives adorning the noodles.

"What do you think?" he asks, offering me a bite.

It's delicious. It's as good as anything I serve here every day—but it needs a little something.

He seems to think so, too; as he swallows his own bite of pasta, we both reach for the same thing—the crushed red pepper.

Martin sprinkles a bit on the top of the pasta, then impulsively leans forward and kisses me, hard and deep, his tongue probing my mouth.

I hold back a moan, immediately thinking about everything that we did last night. And on the plane. And all the things we haven't done yet.

"There," he says, batting his ginger lashes as he picks up the plate in both hands. "Since you needed a little spice."

I follow him as he carries the tray out to the old man and sets it on the table; I join him as he takes a few steps back, watching him take a nibble.

"You there," the old man calls, pointing an age-spotted finger in my direction. "You own the place?"

"I do." I wish I'd put on the crisp black collared shirt I wear at work. You should always look professional. "Is there something I can help you with?"

"You're Erik? Erik Svensson?" the old man clarifies. He's less of a jolly old man and more of a wrinkled bulldog many years past his prime—there's a fierceness in his watery eyes that I can't shake.

"Yes," I say, keeping my voice down so I don't alarm Martin. "Can I help you?"

"My son is—" he starts, and then there's a horrible sound as he gasps for air.

He waves his hands, eyes wide with panic, and does the international, unmistakable motion that means he's choking.

Oh, God, now I have a patron choking in my restaurant.

I've been trained for this. But before I can jump into action, a firm voice comes from behind me.

"Move." Martin charges past me. He's thorough and calm, and pulls the old man out of the booth, wrapping his arms around his middle.

A few jumps, a few grunts, and a green olive shoots out of the old man's mouth, spinning on the tabletop before coming to a slow stop.

The old man gasps and sucks in air, and Martin falls backward away from him, panting.

"Holy shit," I say, putting my arms around his waist to steady him. "You saved his life."

"I wasn't going to let my puttanesca kill a man," he says drily.

The old man takes a minute to catch his breath and then departs, leaving a cash tip that has me reeling.

A stack of hundreds.

"You take it," I say, pushing it toward Martin. "You're the one who saved his life."

"You take it," he retorts, pushing it back. "It's your restaurant."

Eventually, we split it, half to the staff on duty and half to Martin. I tell him he can buy me dinner after the Chef-Off.

And with that, it's time to head back to the airport to catch our flight to Vegas.

What a whirlwind fucking day.

This sobers Martin, and as we get back in the car for the airport, I ask him if he's all right.

"Just... tomorrow," is all he says, and I understand completely.

"Yes. Tomorrow."

Tomorrow, we will compete in the last challenge of the competition.

Tomorrow, we will finally find out who's going to take home that check.

The flight's impossibly fast, and now we're in a rental car from Las Vegas airport headed for Martin's apartment. The whole time, I'm thinking about what I really want to say—that no matter what happens, we'll work it out. The most important thing is that we are honest with each other and cheer each other on. That sort of thing.

But when I walk Martin to the door of his apartment complex, I brush the copper curls back from his face, and all my words leave me.

I press my lips against his.

"See you tomorrow," I say, reluctantly leaving his side.

"May the best man win," Martin adds, and then he opens the door, glancing back at me with a hint of sadness in his eyes—a sadness I can't look away from.

This should be a happy thing—we both made it all the way to the final of this competition, which means that one of us is going to walk away with ten million dollars.

And we've found each other. Surely that's worth more than even that kind of prize.

It hits me that I'm in over my head. That this is way past lust or a competition trauma-bonding fling. I'm fucking falling in love with this man.

But even after fighting through those other challenges, working my ass off to ensure a spot in this final round of competition, I can't stop thinking about all the possible scenarios tomorrow.

I know one thing is for sure—the competition isn't the only thing I'll fight for.

I'll do whatever it takes to save my restaurant from the mob—but I'll fight even harder for Martin.

He's worth way more than ten million dollars.

And even if I lose tomorrow. Maybe it's time my dreams took a different shape anyways.

"Hey," I call just before Martin slips inside. "Wait."

Martin pauses, and I dash back to his side; without hesitating, I grab his face in my hands and kiss him with everything I've got.

I don't want anything to change between us—but I know that tomorrow, it will.

Maybe we should live in this moment a little while longer.

"Come up." I follow him back into his apartment, to his bedroom.

I undress him slowly, savoring his heavenly body, the feel of his skin under my hands, and when he's completely naked, I push him backward onto the bed, his legs falling open.

I'm absolutely breathless when I look at him; he's so beautiful, every inch of him. How did I get this lucky, get to be the man that touches him this way?

"You don't have to," Martin suddenly murmurs, and when I glance up at his face, he's got fear and uncertainty in his eyes.

Fuck.

Did other men he's dated and been with appreciate him? Appreciate him the way I am doing in this moment? He's a fucking god, and as much as I don't want to think about him being with any other guy, I want to think that any time he's been intimate with someone, he's been worshipped. But something makes me think they made him feel unwanted, that they were takers but not givers.

I want to blow them all out of the water.

I kiss the inside of his thigh and whisper, "I want to. I want to do this. Please, let me worship you."

Martin leans his head back, and I kneel down, burying my face between his legs.

Lightly and slowly, I trace my tongue around his tight asshole, relishing in his glorious warm skin. He's grabbing at my hair and trying to pull me up to hurry things along—but I take my time. I flicker my tongue at his rosy hole, delighting in the way he squirms with pleasure, and then I back away again.

Martin's hand flys down to his cock to stroke while I make love to him, but I won't let him come so easily—I want to savor him. I hold his hands at his sides.

Remember that flight earlier today? Yeah, me too, baby boy.

I'm taking my time.

I want every inch of his body to be on fire before he comes.

"Fuck," he mutters, and bucks his hips forward.

Again, I maneuver my tongue all around his asshole, keeping my rhythm on his silky skin steady and consistent. I lick him until he reaches a tipping point, and when he suddenly snaps up to sitting, his hands finding my hair, holding my head still, I know I've done it.

He can't take anymore. He's going wild, and I keep my tongue lapping at his hole—he's stunning, he's everything I've ever wanted. His cock throbs; he's moaning, and then he's reaching desperately for his own dick.

Instead I push his hands away and take his member deep into my own throat. He bucks beneath me, driving himself further and further into my mouth until I taste his salty cum and feel it dribble from my lips.

Martin's hands pull me up and I kiss his mouth. "You're amazing," I whisper to him. "I love seeing you come apart like that."

"Please," he whispers back, and his blue eyes are shining as they find mine. "Take me again. Fuck me."

I don't need to be told twice—I unwrap a condom and roll it onto my already hard cock, and when I lube it and bury it deep in his quivering asshole, my entire body shudders in pleasure.

He feels so fucking amazing, like he was tailor-made to fit me—I thrust in and out of him, enjoying the view—he's spread-eagled in front of me on the bed, his knees pushed up to his shoulders, his pink cock already getting hard again.

I work him up to another orgasm, stroking his cock to make him explode in my fingers, and this time I join him—my orgasm rages through me, and I let out a primal growl as I finish.

God, it hits me that I'd give up ten million dollars to get to be able to do this forever.

When both of us are able to breathe again, I kiss his forehead and get dressed, then pull a light blanket over his delicate form, squeezing his ass one more time for the road.

Then I head back to the hotel, my thoughts swirling in the dark, my heart tugging me in multiple directions.

No, that's a lie—my heart only wants one thing now.

To have a night like this every night for the rest of my life.

But first, I need to cook one more challenge.

CHAPTER TWELVE

MARTIN

The day of the competition, and I'm ready.

This is it.

The finals of the Chow Channel's Chef-Off competition, and I made it to the top two.

There's going to be another challenge.

There's going to be a live audience.

There's going to be a ten-million-dollar check and in less than two hours, that check is going to be handed to either Erik or me.

I should be proud of myself.

I *am* proud of myself.

But also, I'm a scattered mess of nerves and uncertainty as I swipe lip balm on and tie my lucky bandana around my curls in the dressing room.

Erik and I have danced around each other for years now, and it took this cooking competition for us to finally get together—but what if it fizzles after this?

What if I win the money and Erik is so upset at losing, that he can't see me anymore?

What if he wins the money and just disappears?

Done with me forever?

I never thought about this Chef-Off competition as a potentially negative thing in my life until this moment, but I can now see it could start a ripple effect of unwanted consequences—but couldn't a guy without any formal cooking training win ten million bucks and a bright future for himself, his mentor, and maybe even win a future in peace for the man he loves?

Loves?

I get chills just at the thought, but I push the idea down. Soon, I'll have to face this. One way or another. But for now, I need to focus.

As I stare at my face in the dressing room mirror, I remind myself of two things.

I auditioned for this competition to start with—not for myself, but for Frank.

Frank, my mentor.

Frank, who's been more than just that—he's been like a father to me.

He deserves to retire and be able to live a good life, get the best treatments, and retire like he wants.

And I want to give him that. He's given me so much.

Whatever it takes, I'll fight for Frank.

But I remind myself of something else, too. I'm allowed to fight for myself. I'm allowed to chase after what I want—even if that means I'm the least-qualified, or the least-confident person doing it.

And what I want is Erik.

My phone buzzes, and my stomach flutters. I haven't heard from Erik yet, so I'm expecting a text from him.

Instead, it's from Chris.

GOOD LUCK, KIDDO, he writes, and I smile.

He's out there in the audience today, which makes me happy—he's such a good reminder of how far I've come, beating difficult odds to get to this level of skill in my chosen profession.

But his text also reminds me that I need to talk to him about Erik. Let him know what's going on between Erik and me before Chris accidentally sees us kiss or something.

Let him know that things might be getting serious.

My stomach flips upside-down. I hope there will be more kisses with Erik. Something about the way we left things last night—like we were both heading off to war—has me worried.

One last check in the mirror, one last check of my apron string, and I'm ready.

"Knock, knock." Someone comes into my dressing room without waiting for me to answer, and as soon as I see who it is, my skin crawls.

It's Anthony. He's in another one of his expensive-looking suits, and he clasps his hands together, perusing me up and down.

"Oh, you look the part, all dolled up in your little uniform. Are you nervous for the big show?"

I am nervous, yes, but not just because of the live audience. I'm nervous because my entire life could change today, in more ways than one—but I'm not about to share this with a freaking mobster.

"A little," I tell him, just to get him to leave. My voice stays neutral. "I'm just going to grab some water before we're due on set. Thanks for stopping by." I move toward the door, trying to keep an innocent smile on my face, but Anthony blocks me.

"I've got something much better than a drink of water," he insists, and my insides squirm as he pushes me backward with a firm hand on my chest and storms past me into my dressing room.

"Oh, come on, kid, what's the matter?" he chides when I flinch at his touch. "We both know just what kind of guy you are. Look at you. You're a real fruit. And I know exactly what kind of stuff guys like you are willing to do to get ahead in life."

This time, Anthony slides his hand down my back, and is just about to reach my ass, when I clench my fist and take a step back.

"Don't touch me again," I hiss. I'm ready to throw a punch. It'll hurt the hell out of my hand, but I don't care.

Anthony's smirk is infuriating, and he reaches for me again. "What's a matter? You only like blonds?"

But I don't have to hit him.

Someone else does.

Erik, holding a bouquet of the most gorgeous spring wildflowers I've ever seen, steps into my dressing room and without hesitating, slugs Anthony squarely in the nose.

"Oh, shit!" I cry.

Oh, shit is right.

Anthony stumbles back, crashing into the wall, his hands flying up to catch the blood that begins to pour down onto his luxury suit, onto his pristine white shirt.

There's a fucking mobster with a broken nose bleeding half to death, and I couldn't give a shit less.

I immediately rush into Erik's arms, covering him with grateful kisses.

"I don't know what happened!" the words come out in a rush. "I was in here getting ready, and he just pushed his way in."

"It's all right," Erik tells me. "I'm just glad you're okay." He's gazing at me with such adoration in those pale blue eyes of his, I don't notice a third person joining us in my dressing room.

My brother, Chris.

Oh, my God. My whole body freezes, unsure how this is going to go.

"First of all, what the hell is going on here?" he asks, gesturing to the way I'm tangled in his best friend's arms.

"And second, which one of you punched the mobster?"

The producers question us all, and we all say the same things—me, Chris, Erik, even Anthony confesses to coming into my dressing room uninvited, though he, of course, defends his decision to grope me without consent.

"This homo came onto me," he says flatly as a responder presses ice packs against his nose. "I'm not that kinda guy."

It sounds so rote that it makes the whole thing more chilling. This guy is literally a psychopath.

I want to punch him again for this response—as if the sight of me, terrified, hunched over, backing into the corner of my dressing room where I was alone and vulnerable was some kind of an invitation.

Then anger flares. Asshole.

Erik's icing his hand, too, which is already all black and blue from his epic punch—and then the producer comes to deliver the bad news.

"We can't let you compete," he tells Erik. "There are strict rules about fighting and inciting violence between contestants. I'm sorry. You'll have to forfeit."

The host, Rodney, turns to me with a wide grin plastered on his face. "Hey, that means you're the de facto winner. Congratulations!"

I'm shocked as the rest of the people in the room start to congratulate me, shaking my hand, walking right past Erik as if he's some thug and not the man who just saved me from a full-on assault.

They're ready to give me the prize.

On one hand, this moment is everything I hoped for—ten million dollars. They can be mine, if I would just reach out and take the prize.

Enough to buy the Wish Café from Frank, ensuring his retirement.

Enough to turn Frank's old place into the restaurant of my dreams.

I look at Erik, who stares resolutely at the floor, devastated. He gives me one quick look with a genuinely happy smile, and I understand its meaning—that I don't have to worry about losing him.

If I decide the competition's over, here and now, and I take this money, Erik will still want me. He'll stand by my side, and he'll punch a hundred more Mafia dudes if it means we can be together.

But I let my gaze go past him.

Out in the audience, I see a familiar face, sitting halfway up the bleachers.

Waiting patiently for the competition to begin so he can watch his prizewinning cook, his protégée.

Frank.

Frank's come to see me compete.

I've never been handed anything in my life—and I sure don't want to start now.

"No," I say. "No. Let him compete. I want to win this fair and square. And he didn't punch a fellow contestant—he defended me against someone coming into my dressing room uninvited. He should be rewarded for doing the security guards' job, if you ask me."

The producers look a little surprised by this, but they whisper to each other, then turn back to me. "We're just not sure if it's the right message to send."

"Let him compete." The voice is thick with a Japanese accent, and the figure standing with his arms crossed is the very epitome of righteous authority.

Hiroko, the judge, his face stern, his eyes thoughtful. "He deserves to have a fair shot. Both of them do."

It shouldn't feel this way, but Hiroko's insistence that Erik should cook feels like one more blow to Anthony Napali. The producers all nod in agreement, and Erik stands up, kissing me joyfully.

"Let's go," he says with a waggle of his eyebrows and then frowns, seeing Chris right behind me.

"Good luck, you two." Chris pulls me into one last hug and whispers, "We're going to talk about that kiss later."

Fine with me. There's plenty of time to hash out details about my relationship with Erik later.

Right now, though, it's time to cook.

CHAPTER THIRTEEN

ERIK

"Are you ready?"

Rodney riles up the crowd, getting them to cheer over and over for the cameras that pan around the kitchen, showing the huge audience.

"On your marks!"

The theme's been announced—we have to bake cakes.

Cakes. Dessert. My weakest category.

"Get set!"

Beside me, Martin catches my eye and the grin on his face is breathtaking. It's a grin that tells me to give it all I've got. It's a grin that tells me we're a team, even though we're facing off against each other for a sum of money so massive, I can't even fathom seeing that amount on a check.

It's a grin that tells me we've both already won, no matter what.

"Cook!"

An alarm buzzes, and I rush off into the pantry to collect my ingredients.

"When's the last time you made a cake?" I mutter to Martin, hoping he'll join me in griping about this choice of theme, but he smirks and says, "Last week," before skipping off to the fruit.

Well, fuck.

Might as well have fun with it if I'm about to lose in front of a live audience.

I've never been great with baking, but I channel everything I have, everything I know into this one cake.

I mix up the batter, the roar of the crowd drowning out my doubts, and get it into the oven.

I beat my frosting—that's not a metaphor, although I do think about what I'm going to do with Martin and some homemade frosting later—tasting it every few minutes to make sure it's the right balance between sweet and tart.

I let my cakes cool, stacking the layers, adding a healthy amount of frosting to it all, and I decorate it just as the ending buzzer sounds.

Here's what I made, inspired entirely by Martin:

A triple layer vanilla lemon rosemary cake.

Triple layers, because I can't get enough of him.

Vanilla, because he's sweet and comforting.

Lemon, because he can be tart and sassy.

Rosemary, because there's an edge to him that is smart and unexpected.

And I frost it in that trendy naked style, where half the cake is exposed, because, well… because I love seeing him naked.

But I don't tell any of this to the judges when I present the cake.

I simply say, "Bon appetit," and watch them dig in.

My cake is not nearly as pretty as Martin's—he's made a pink champagne cake, decorated with soft pale pink candied rose petals and the inside layers are gradient, shifting from dark hot pink up to white.

It looks sumptuous and delicious and so I'm not at all surprised when the judges all frown, lost in deliberation.

It's going to be a tough call, but as the audience settles and quiets and the host is given the envelope with the final scores, I hold Martin's hands. Both of them.

I don't need ten million bucks to face down the mob.

Screw that. I'll do it with Martin at my side.

"And the winner is…" Rodney waits for the drumroll to say the name, and I practically mouth it along with him: "Martin Slade!"

Confetti bursts out of cannons. The audience cheers, and somewhere in the seats, I see Frank McIntosh himself, standing up out of his wheelchair to clap for his protégé.

"You did it!" I shout as I pull Martin in for a celebratory kiss. I'm genuinely happy for him—he truly deserves it.

Once the press has gotten all the photos they need of the winner and most of the audience has left, they turn on the lights in the casino's event arena and Martin squints, peering behind me at someone lurking just offstage.

"Don't panic," he says, his own eyes looking frantic as he clutches my hand, "but it's your old Mafia friend, Anthony."

I don't panic, but I'll be lying if I say I'm not pissed off.

My adrenaline surges as Anthony walks toward us, his face bruised and swollen. "Relax," he says, "I just wanted to congratulate the winner."

I stand protectively in front of Martin. "You keep your hands where I can see them," I say through clenched teeth. "Unless you want to go for round two."

Anthony narrows his eyes. "You don't want to mess with me," he says. "You have no idea who I am."

"Actually, I do." Something about being near Martin makes me bolder than I ever am alone. "I know who you are, and I know what you're doing with The Shark Fin. And it ends now."

Anthony raises his eyebrows. "Is that right? And who is going to stop me?"

"I am." The voice comes from the audience. Martin and I glance out at the only person left in the bleachers, and Martin covers his mouth with his hands, shocked.

"No," he murmurs to himself. "That can't be the same man."

I whisper, "Fuck," under my breath. It is the same man —the old man who visited The Shark Fin that day in Boston, that man who choked and nearly died... until Martin saved his ass.

He's here, in the audience.

In another Hawaiian shirt, to boot.

And as he makes his way down the bleachers, Anthony chortles and rolls his eyes. "What are you doing here, Pa, huh?"

"Pa?" I mouth to Martin whose eyes are wide as we eavesdrop.

"Chasing after you, apparently, shithead," the old man retorts, and extends a hand to me. "Sal Napali. Father to this one who can't seem to stay out of trouble."

His accent sounds vaguely Italian, and a silver scar streaks across his cheek, giving him a menacing look. But he turns to Martin and says, "Congratulations to you, young man. What an achievement, and what a chunk of change. You have any plans for your big win?"

Martin shifts his feet, uncomfortably looking at Anthony, but Anthony seems to have tempered his behavior quite a bit in the presence of his father—I almost laugh but manage to keep my cool.

Even mobsters are afraid of something, it seems.

"Yes, actually." Martin lifts up his chin, glancing at Sal as he speaks. "I'm going to buy out your son's investment in The Shark Fin."

"What?" Anthony spits. "No, you're not. That's ridiculous. Erik, tell your little boyfriend how ridiculous this is—"

"I'm going to buy out all the investors," Martin goes on, "so Erik's free to run his business without any outside influence."

He chooses his words very carefully, peering at Sal as he speaks so he knows exactly what he's referring to.

I hold my breath, trying to keep myself from arguing with him. It's his money and he should be spending it on himself, and not on me, but I'm also trying to keep from kissing him, since it's the most romantic gesture anyone's ever made for me.

Ever.

Sal inspects Martin up and down, his shrewd eyes narrowed, then seems to decide something, nodding to himself. He shakes his head and his bulldog jowls give a satisfying wobble.

"No," he tells Martin. "You're not going to do that. You're not going to spend a dime paying back any of those investors. Those are all my boys—Anthony, Guido, Benny."

I jerk my head up. Benny's one of the gang, too? Well, shit. I had no idea.

"Those are my boys, and they're all going to walk away, no questions asked. No more money flowing in or out of Erik's place, you understand me? You walk away." Sal directs this last statement to his son, who looks like he's going to protest, but instead slumps and nods in weak agreement.

"You seem like good people," Sal goes on, "and what's more, you saved my life. So, we're even. Enjoy your money and enjoy your restaurant. Oh, and don't worry about this one," he finishes, grabbing his son by the collar of his shirt.

"I'll be keeping a tighter leash on him. Come on, Anthony. Let's have a chat about how we treat business associates with proper respect."

I wait until the two Napalis are really, truly gone, then I let out a whoop of celebration so loud, it echoes off the ceiling of the conference center. I'm free.

Truly free.

And what's more, I'm walking away from the Chow Channel's Chef-Off competition with the best prize I could win—a man I love.

"So, now what are you going to do with all that cash, moneybags?" I tease Martin after we've packed up our things and we're walking down the front steps of the casino, out onto Las Vegas boulevard. "Retirement for Frank? Early retirement for you? A whole set of fancy new wine glasses?"

Martin pauses, his mouth pouting in deep thought. "What if you sell The Shark Fin?"

I frown but listen as he continues.

"You have a life in Boston, and I don't want to push you out of there," he says carefully. "But what if you moved up here with me? What if you sold your place, and I'll buy the Wish Café from Frank, and we collaborate on something completely new? Something that's all ours, no investors, no outside opinions, just the two of us building a menu, cooking together?"

I don't even have to think about it.

I know my answer right away.

Fuck, yes.

But instead of speaking, I grab Martin and tug him into my arms, giving him a long, deep kiss. I've waited so long to have him by my side, and now that he's here, I can hardly believe he's mine.

"I can't wait to get started," I tell him, and the two of us head toward my hotel, on our way to the rest of our lives.

EPILOGUE

ERIK

"All right, everyone, you know the drill. Taste test. We need to figure out what's going on our menus."

Martin and I are standing at the head of a long table filled with our closest friends and family.

Chris is on the other end, grinning as he listens to his new girlfriend talk about how much she loves the décor—he softened about me and Martin after Sal promised the Mafia would stay out of our affairs.

I think the new girlfriend has helped, too. She's melted his icy heart.

We're in our brand-new restaurant, two weeks from opening, and we're still trying to finalize the last details. The location is great—we've taken over the spot where the Wish Café used to be, and Frank McIntosh took the cash from the sale and moved into a gorgeous apartment on the Common. He's set up to spend the rest of his days enjoying the park, enjoying visits from his celebrity friends, and eating at some of the best restaurants nearby.

And of course, unlimited eats at our new place anytime he wants.

"We're going to present these to you blind," Martin continues, glancing at me as he speaks, "and you just tell us which one you like better."

His hand's laced in mine, and I run my thumb over the ring that encircles his left ring finger. I proposed to him on the night we signed the paperwork for the restaurant. One huge life change wasn't enough.

And frankly, I had to fight to wait that long.

Every part of me wanted this man as my husband. All to myself, all mine, for the rest of forever.

Lucky for me, he said yes.

Actually, he said fuck yes and we christened Wish Café in some interesting ways that night. Six times.

As soon as the restaurant is up and running, we'll plan our wedding—but for now, we have a serious kink to figure out: whose recipes are going to be on our menu?

"Care to make this a little more interesting?" I say, and Martin raises one eyebrow. "Loser makes the winner anything they want in the kitchen. Chocolate soufflé, beef bourguignon, six-hour enchiladas, anything."

"Does it have to be in the kitchen?" Martin asks. "Or can it be the bedroom?"

This sends a shiver licking down my spine, and my cock hardens—but while I'm fantasizing about what I'd request from Martin if I should win, he passes out the covered dishes and instructs everyone to lift the lids and eat.

I'm praying I win, and it has nothing to do with chef pride. I can't keep my eyes off the gorgeous, sexy redhead next to me—or my mind from imagining what I'll be requesting when I win.

Hell, to be fair, I'll probably be winning even if I lose, if the wicked gleam in his eyes is any indication.

I've prepared a selection of dishes I think should go on our new menu—simple garlic bread bites topped with mussels, sashimi with fresh ginger, lime ceviche. And I'm pretty proud of my concoctions until I see what Martin's made.

His dishes pop with color and vitality. He's made fish tacos topped with red cabbage and mangos, a crab gazpacho with avocado, mixed seafood egg rolls with cilantro.

Everything is mouthwatering, inventive but familiar, using seasonal ingredients that will keep our supply list low-cost and our profit margins large—so it's no surprise when everyone votes for Martin's menu items over mine.

And yet, he's managed to do it while still bringing my passion for seafood to the forefront.

Of course, he has.

"All right," I tell him after we finish our meal with our friends and we're scrubbing the dishes. "You're the big winner. What do you want?"

Martin looks me up and down, that dimple appearing in the corner of his cheek. "I saw you kneading that garlic bread earlier. My shoulders are a little sore. I want a massage."

I grin. Knowing Martin, it's going to start as a massage and end as something much naughtier—but I pretend it's all business as I nod in agreement. "Deal," I say.

"**A**re you ready?" I call into our bedroom in Martin's Las Vegas apartment, and Martin affirms that, yes, he's ready. We're going to be moving into a bigger place soon, but we've made some fantastic memories here.

I come in—

And I'm utterly unprepared for the sexy view that awaits me.

Martin's completely naked, lying face down on the bed. His ass is gloriously firm and supple, and I know that if I spank it, it'll jiggle and bounce ever so slightly and look so tantalizing, I won't be able to resist it—but fair is fair.

He won the taste test, so now I must deliver the goods.

"Can I start on your shoulders?" I ask, and Martin murmurs something that sounds like assent.

I work my hands along his slender shoulders, down his back—he has such creamy soft skin, and I work up quite an appetite myself as I touch him.

Moving down his back, I try to make my kneading as gentle as possible, working out the very real knots in his muscles; being a chef is tough work, and there's evidence of how hard he's been working all over his back. I pretend his body is dough, kneading it, squeezing it, with all the love and care I have, and then I slide further down.

Martin lets out a soft groan, and when I peer at him, I see he's got one hand under him, rubbing her cock as I massage. Fuck, my own cock gets hard.

"Lower," Martin commands, the hint of a grin in his voice, and suddenly I understand what this is—he's trying to tease me. That's what the real prize is—not getting all his knots worked out with my expert hands but seeing how far he can push me until I snap with my own lust.

My hands squeeze his butt, and I take in the sight of his small but round cheeks—whatever he was hoping for, he was right. I can't take it anymore.

Touching him is making me hard enough to rocket off into space. It's a familiar thing, but I have to fuck him now, hard enough to see that tight little ass bounce with my thrusting.

"Come on," I tug him by the hips so he's up on his knees, and I rip down my pants, releasing my stiffened length, lubing it up and positioning it right at his opening.

He slides down the length, sheathing me inside him, and grinding in just the way he does that feels so epic.

It feels so good when I fill him up—Martin arches his back, meeting my every move. I reach forward and grab a handful of his beautiful red curls, feeling his head jerk back in my grasp. He strokes his cock until he convulses with pleasure, and his body milks an orgasm out of me.

God, I love this beautiful man, and he's all mine.

We both finish, wrapped in each other's arms, as we fall asleep on top of the blankets. I can't stop thinking about how lucky I am.

The Chow Channel will air the Chef-Off Competition in a few weeks, the perfect timing for our restaurant opening.

And in fact, we've been invited to do a pop-up restaurant tomorrow that promises to be a good time.

I get to work every day with my best friend Chris, who we hired as the restaurant manager—he was over the desk job and excited to relocate to Las Vegas since his girlfriend's out here—and my fiancé, the most handsome, brilliant person I've ever known.

Most importantly, we have a whole cupboard full of wine glasses, and now we get to live happily ever after —one day at a time.

It's a life worth way more than ten million bucks.

Some things—the best things—are fucking priceless.

Be the first to find out about all of Dillon Hart's new releases, book sales, and freebies by joining his VIP Mailing List. Join today and get a FREE book -- instantly! Join by clicking here!

ABOUT THE AUTHOR

Dillon Hart, who lives in San Francisco, writes compelling gay romance novels that embody the essence of love and human relationships. His works are inspired by the diverse communities that call the city home, from the vibrant Castro neighborhood to the bohemian Mission district. In his spare time, Dillon enjoys riding the F Line streetcar from Market Street to Fisherman's Wharf, where he enjoys the ocean breezes and the bustle of the waterfront.

More on www.dillonhart.com

Join my newsletter by clicking here.

Write me at contact@dillonhart.com

FIND ME ON SOCIAL MEDIA